Penguin Books

WHATEVER
❖ HAPPENED ❖
TO ROSIE DUNN?

Tom Beauford, the pseudonym for John Sligo, was born in New Zealand in 1944. After completing his university education at St John's College, Cambridge, he worked for a time at FAO, United Nations, in Rome, and later as a film and television journalist. His articles and criticisms have appeared in newspapers and magazines in Italy, Australia and New Zealand. He has also broadcast for the ABC.

John Sligo has published three other novels: *The Cave* which won the New Zealand PEN Award for the best first novel, *Final Things* which won the NSW Premier's Award and *The Concert Masters*, a political thriller set in Rome.

He is now an Australian citizen and full-time writer with a love of Italian cooking, Jungian psycho-analysis and the Australian criminal mind.

WHATEVER
❖ HAPPENED ❖
TO ROSIE DUNN?

Tom Beauford

Penguin Books

For Suzanne Falkiner and Julian and Trish Canny, who have occasional lapses in taste

Penguin Books Australia Ltd
487 Maroondah Highway, PO Box 257
Ringwood, Victoria, 3134, Australia
Penguin Books Ltd
Harmondsworth, Middlesex, England
Viking Penguin Inc.
40 West 23rd Street, New York, NY 10010, USA
Penguin Books Canada Limited
2801 John Street, Markham, Ontario, Canada, L3R 1B4
Penguin Books (N.Z.) Ltd
182-190 Wairau Road, Auckland 10, New Zealand

First published by Penguin Books Australia, 1989

Typeset in 11pt Bembo by Midland Typesetters Maryborough
Made and printed in Australia by Australian Print Group, Maryborough, Victoria.

Beauford, Tom, 1944–
Whatever happened to Rosie Dunn?

ISBN 0 14 012220 6.

I. Title.

NZ823'.2

✦ PROLOGUE ✦

Father Aquino looked at the large woman who sat in front of him with a glass of wine. While she talked, he took in the lines of fatigue and fear.

Sophie Parnell, investigator, was not easily frightened. She'd seen too much in her job, but he knew the last few days in Thailand had drained her. It came out in the way she spoke, the nervous movement of her fingers as she made a point. And the way, occasionally, she looked at him for support.

She had always had that mannerism, lapsed or practising, and these days, Father Aquino suspected, Sophie had more of a conscience than half the mob that turned up at church for mass. Sophie now played the games by her own rules, and if she strayed now and then, as she was doing, he supposed, with the tough young man who had driven her to the presbytery (Father Aquino had heard the car and checked through the study window), then that was of no great moment.

He listened intently while Sophie built her case, point by point. Admitting, too, part of her reason for taking it on –revenge. But then, as she admitted, revenge somehow never worked out.

Her voice gained strength as she moved into the story, deftly painting for her friend and confidante the portraits of the main characters – Charlie Dunn, Rosie Dunn, Ruth Dunn, Janet Craig and the holiday makers up at Kata Beach.

Then she mentioned Rufus Stone and he noted the bitterness in her face, but held back, with a certain amazed awe. It was not yet time to tell her.

Instead, he looked at the crumpled cotton dress and the sweat marks under her arms. She had come straight from the airport and hadn't gone home first, to change. That pleased Father Aquino, and he smiled.

Sophie noticed and picked up speed, but Father Aquino raised his hand to slow her down. In these matters of conscience there was no rush. He refilled her wineglass.

'And to think,' she said, 'that all this began with a reception on the *Queen Elizabeth*. I'd just finished a case that day, a petty crime as I told you. A good man, really. And that evening Charlie Dunn seemed like an answer to my prayers for money. But if I'd known what I now know, I don't think I would have taken it.'

She finished the story and looked round the study, focussing for a moment on the Gubbio Madonna and its serene, medieval smile.

'I wouldn't have taken it, since I'm facing a person who is evil. Two people, really, who are evil.

'I've been through it all, Father Aquino – drugs, murder, double-cross and now this horror to end it up. And I think I'm in checkmate. I think I've failed.

'Oh, I know what happened to Rosie Dunn, but how can I tell what I know?'

Father Aquino sat for a moment in silence then smiled. 'God has answered you, Sophie. You *can* tell what happened to Rosie Dunn.'

'How?' Sophie looked more drawn than puzzled.

'Wait, I have something to show you,' he said, and left the room.

Sophie Parnell parked her car on Poplar Street in Surry Hills and walked up to Oxford Street. The cars were belching purple high octane exhaust, the pigeons wheeling in the acquamarine sky, the aspirins were working. She took off her dark glasses and grimaced. A block ahead was her destination, standing high over the green swards of Hyde Park and the Bauhaus-Pre-Raphaelite war memorial to the Glorious Dead, whose tourist tripping had left them forever manuring a foreign soil.

Her legs seemed steady enough so she drifted off in her thoughts. Hyde Park! Not at all like its namesake in London that she'd woken up to every day. Then she'd been the usual raw recruit completing her doctorate in lovely Marlowe at London University and working three evenings a week at a pub in Chelsea. The other evenings were devoted to Charles the Pom. In those days Sophie had been, as she now admitted, a degree kleptomaniac. She had already amassed a satisfactory bachelor of law and arts when the scholarship came up. She had grabbed at it without thinking and hadn't since regretted the added labour. On her return, when the taxi drivers had seemed younger, she'd started up a legal practice, but the sleaze and nobility of the soul were lacking. That was the real reason for leaving law and academe for private dickery. Sophie snorted and moaned as a bright white light needled through her cerebellum, and walked through the foyer of the National Equity.

It was eight twenty-five, and how she was this morning could be squarely blamed on Cliff last night. He'd finally packed his bags at three after much wine and accusation.

'Like ya outfit.' Daph Cowlie took Sophie's cigarette to light her own.

Sophie smoothed down the green cotton dress with the flattering line.

Daph looked around the workers. 'Jamey's goin to be late again.'

'Yeah,' Sophie leaned back against the wall, fitting into the part as she had from the beginning of the case. The Rental Bond Board, known to the serfs as the Mental Bond Board, had only one function – to collect bonds on flats, keep them safe while making money out of the interest and return them to either tenant or landlord, depending on who deserved it or was the more crafty in knowing the machinery of demand and supply. Of course, in the middle was the clerk crim who'd been raking off a fair whack in the past six to eight months.

The lifts for floors fourteen to twenty-six were still somewhere up the spout when Jamey arrived in a rush. Sophie smiled at his blond hair, rumpled shirt that needed a press, blue denims and charming twitchy smile. Didn't look as if he'd had much of a night either. She could feel the hunted vibration around him – the pounce, the teeth, all that fur and squealing and blood. Enough to turn the Virgin Mary Buddhist. Jamey, of course, was the clerk crim.

'How are ya feeling, Jamey?' asked Daph.

'OK,' grunted Jamey, balancing on his sneakers, heels low and toes high.

Jamey was from the right kind of family. Daph was from the Western suburbs where long lines of houses spawned more, like a kind of cancer in brick and lawn. Lots of violent men returned there from the pub for a bit of incest or rape.

Westie Cliff had never been like that, just played at being dumb and nasty to get by. Better in his way than David the Marxist intellectual from Glebe. David had read it all, like Charles the Pom in her London days. Could quote pages from Plato's dialogues, although she was the wrong sex for that effort. Cliff didn't know much, couldn't name anything of a lady's charms in correct Latin and just enjoyed himself. The trouble was the afterglow. *Gimme a cig, Soph. Turn on the tele, Soph.* Lying back on the sheets, hirsute and content, the little woman serviced and the world in order.

Where *did* you find a man of all seasons? Sophie sighed and risked a glance at Jamey the crim, soon to be unmasked. In an actual afterglow, there was nothing better than Charles the Pom and David the Marxist and their *ideas* – Donne, Yeats, madrigals. Perfect to complete the ceremonies of the flesh. Alas! Alack! With a conclusion perfect, you were supposed to forget the motor that had ground to a discontented stop before a glow was even rippling around the horizon.

'Bloody lifts!' Daph fished in her bag, brought out a Barbara Cartland and got stuck into reality. Sophie had half-believed in it once. With Charles the Pom and his lovely Eton-Irish accent. Whatever had happened to Charles the Pom? Probably reverted to the boys with the rest of the English upper-class males. School did it, and those dreadful dominant Mums with their Wedgwood voices.

The lights started flickering red, down and down. The doors opened and the cattle stampeded in, leaving the polite Jamey standing back.

The doors opened again and Sophie stepped out on to the yellow carpets and slowed down through the side doors to the open office space: lockers lined up against a wall, desk, telephones and two glassed-in cages. In one, the Big Boss was seated. Probably been there all night, accounts books open, checking figures; checking, rechecking. His Aryan blue eyes and steamroller jaw tightened up as the serfs frolicked about. He'd just arrived, the poor bugger, from the State Treasury and was an economist of minor note. So minor that he was only on thirty-five or forty thousand a year. Which was, by chance, the approximate amount the charming Jamey had purloined.

Jamey had a gambling problem, as his ex-wife Mary had

told Sophie. She'd met Mary by planned accident at a cocktail party two weeks ago. Mary was an easy enough target. Intelligent, neurotic, like all well-brought-up Eastern suburbs girls and ready enough to talk about Jamey after a few drinks: ready to tell her about the house cleaned out of saleable items and Jamey sitting in the middle of the scene weeping about his gambling binge. Looking for comfort and getting it until finally Mary had walked out for good. Jamey had gone to a bedsit in Kings Cross.

Jamey ran the happiest section in the office. He took cash bonds across the counter. The client was given his receipt, and Jamey simply forgot to give the receipt and money to Accounts. He was now looking for comfort from Lulu James.

Lulu worked on phones next to the counter section, and Sophie could see her messed-about red mop and the crim's blond hair close together. Jamey was a charmer and Lulu in her earth mother role could sublimate quite nicely. Lulu's face was soft and confiding, asking for confession. But she couldn't know yet that Jamey was the man. That Jamey had left all the stolen receipts in his locker. The locker left unlocked. There was something about the little boy in Jamey.

Sophie made her decision at the end of morning tea break. She went back to the counter and made a quick private phone call to Jamey's wife.

The day passed towards four o'clock and closing time. The last customer was an old Greek biddy, haunches firm in regulation black with thick swollen ankles encased in solid brown stockings. One of the good landladies . . . 'They young people,' she hissed at Sophie, one respectable woman to another, 'they not marry, they do things on carpet. I know. Also, smoking of drugs and break up house with party and they burn curtain and call me ugly words.'

Sophie leaned forward to take it all in but was blasted back by the garlic. Nice old cow, she decided.

Sophie went to her locker. She'd never kept anything much there, so the clean-out wasn't obvious. The Big Boss was glancing her way, but then he wasn't her Big Boss. She'd been employed by a Higher Authority. An old mate from the legal profession, now a bureaucrat, too. The Big Boss hadn't liked that at all. That and Sophie being a qualified lawyer with too many contacts. Couldn't understand her. Why wasn't she socially upwardly mobile? It was like the profanation of the sacrament. She hadn't opened her mouth and accepted.

Sophie glanced around the office, sorry in a way she couldn't come clean. But that wasn't on. Not yet.

She went down in the lift with Daph and some of the boys. All were hitting the pub across the street for the Happy Hour. It would be thick there tonight, she reflected.

Jamey headed off along Oxford Street. He'd be going home to wait for Mary, who'd rung, on Sophie's instructions, to make an appointment with him.

Back at the car, the traffic police had been busy. Sophie got in and drove off.

It wasn't that Jamey shouldn't suffer a bit, she thought, but not at Long Bay Gaol. Jamey boy was just too good looking. To survive he'd wheel and deal, and for safety become the nancy of a Big Boy. That was what the Big Boss up there would be anticipating for him. Nothing precise, mind you, but punishment for all his sleepless nights. Jamey boy suffering, being hunted to the dock and maybe, just before the trial, throwing himself over the Gap as he had once thought of doing, according to Mary.

That place had claimed a few, including her own cousin, Rosie. The inquest was sometime soon, she remembered. She hadn't seen Charlie Dunn, Rosie's father, for an age, he being the successful side of the family.

Sophie parked her blue, ancient Volkswagon in Macleay Street. It was still early for Kings Cross, and the junkies didn't go for anything under a Mitsubishi. She picked up her Peruvian shopping basket, noted one of the handles was again coming unstuck and made her way along tinsel land. Being the centre of vice and pleasure, it was well policed so that the due processes of profit could go on.

The chrome, light, music, blared equally. The arcades were doing good business with the poker machines and space games.

5

The dealers would be starting to work, and some of the girls were waiting in the doorways.

Sophie turned into the alley where the porn shops sold the usual videos and sexual turn-ons, and where a clairvoyant hung out. Arabic music came from the Lebanese take-away. Sophie felt her stomach rumbling and realised she hadn't eaten today. She took the two steps needed off the pavement and glanced at the metal containers with the houmous and tabouli, the pressed meat rotating on the spit. She gave her order and paid.

'You want chilli powder, Miss?'

Sophie nodded.

The falafel was expertly rolled and the coffee poured.

Mary arrived.

Sophie, still eating, put her private detective licence on the table. Mary got her glasses and peered at it and giggled. She handed it back.

'Do you make a living at it?'

Sophie lit up a cigarette and ignored the question. When she had finished filling Mary in, Mary cried briefly and then pulled herself together.

They walked down thirty yards of the alley and into Jamey's building. Mary held her briefcase tight. 'I don't know how he can live around here. With all these *junkies*. I'd be frightened to come home at night.'

'Material,' said Sophie austerely. 'He'll get a good novel if he ever writes one.'

'Yes, I suppose so.' Mary patted at her hair as they reached Jamey's front door. Outside, a bag of garbage was giving off an unpleasant smell.

Mary knocked.

The door was opened.

Mary marched in, stopped like a soldier on parade, and sat in one of the two easy chairs.

Sophie wandered through to the kitchenette, found three glasses and returned. She poured the drinks, handed them around, took out her licence and gave it to Jamey. Jamey glanced at it then grew frozen and vacant, as if his skull had opened on to a long, low, dark wasteland.

'Sorry about the mess,' he said in Mary's direction, handing back the licence to Sophie.

Mary put down her briefcase, stared at the soft brown leather and began to blubber noisily. 'How could you?' she got out between sobs. 'You said it would never happen again. Why?'

'I don't know,' said Jamey, looking at the blue felt carpet.

Sophie topped up their whiskies.

'I'm here to give due warning,' she said.

'You're still so bloody lucky, Jamey.' Mary suddenly swigged down the whisky.

Jamey didn't doubt her and gave Sophie a straight glance.

'On Monday, my report and evidence will be on the desk of the State Attorney.'

'What should I do?' He looked like a boy caught stealing apples.

Sophie felt that dreadful maternal contraction in her womb that immediately went to work on her feelings.

'You see,' Sophie was gentle, 'the State hates getting ripped off. If you don't get in first with your confession you'll be down for a minimum of four years and no parole. So you've got to show you're penitent.

'It's like the inquisition, Jamey luv. You've denied fundamental doctrine. It's worse than rape or murder or interfering with a kid. It hits right at the nerve centre of tinsel land. So it's sackcloth and ashes. Confession of heresy. Pleas for mercy, back bared for the penitential lash! That way you justify *them* since you saw the error of your ways. You confessed before they knew because you know they are *right*.'

'Thanks, Soph.' Jamey took Mary's hand and they faced her together. 'I'll ring up my old man, he knows one of the senior detectives at the Darlinghurst station.'

Mary began to tidy up the room, looking as if she had done it before. Folding clothes, smoothing down the greying sheets.

Neither of them seemed to notice Sophie leaving.

2

Paddington was ten minutes by car from the Cross and a world away in social aspirations.

Ten years ago Sophie had bought a terrace in Regent Street. Now the area was full of trendies, neurotic in their need for Victorian iron lace balconies, smart interiors and landscaped gardens to provide a setting for their aerobics-trimmed bodies and pastel designer clothes. The street was full of Renaults and hatch-backs. Californian lifestyle creeping up the drainpipe like damp, she thought.

It was also a world away from the National Equity and Daph, who would be pissed by now at the pub or rocketing homewards to chops and a night with the tele. A world away, too, from Jamey boy and his grey sheets.

She pulled into the kerb. Of course, the reason she lived here was obvious. It reminded her of London. Not Kangaroo Valley where the Poms still thought Dame Ednas and Kennys hung out drinking Fosters, but some of the squares of Chelsea and Knightsbridge. It was just as beautiful on this late summer evening. It lacked a nightingale, that was true, but a mob of sulphur-crested cockatoos had flown over from Centennial Park, raucous overbearing lot that they were. Two talked down to her while another three hung around her chimney pot screeching to the world's generality.

Sitting on her front doorstep was Harry Bowers, TV anchorman, critic, film producer, director, poet, ex-lover.

Sophie did a double take and remembered she'd meant to put the date in her diary.

'Sorry, mate,' she called out, slamming the car door. 'I got held up. Business.'

'Treating you well?' asked Harry, standing up.

Harry was close to forty but admitted a mature thirty-seven for publicity. He had greying hair and a wide grin with white teeth.

Sophie smoothed down his kiss curl and put the key in the lock. 'Just completed a case, Harry. Grand larceny, and all my sympathy with the crim again.'

She walked into the hall and Harry did a smart left turn and slumped down in an armchair in the renovated front room. Sophie paused to admire the effect of cream armchairs, red Nepalese rugs, a large fern, bookcases and Harry.

Harry pretended to admire the Brett Whiteley painting, a gift from a grateful client which Sophie felt obliged to display.

Sophie made for the stairs, carpeted but needing a shampoo.

The rest of the house was semi-done. A bit, thought Harry, like Sophie herself. Always in extension; a marvellous muddle of styles.

Sophie in the unrenovated bathroom stepped into the shower closet, pulled on the shower cap and turned on the taps. Cliff, she saw, had forgotten to take his razor and, on the window ledge, his aftershave. She soaped and cleaned, and as usual, rifled through her operatic repertoire. This time *La Bohème*, Mimi meeting Rudolfo. *Mi chiamo Mimi, ma mio nome è Lucia*, down to the hacking cough. Harry knew the opera since he'd directed it a couple of years ago in a notable flop, panned by critics and public alike.

'Wonderful,' called out Harry, lying, 'but you'd better get your act together or the food will be gone.'

'I'll do it in me next incarnation, Harr,' said Sophie in her Cockney voice. 'La Stupenda of Star Wars. The Cosmic Soprano.'

'You're a bloody bass, Soph.'

Sophie grabbed for the towel, dried herself and edged past

the scales installed by Cliffie. 'Since when could you tell one voice from another?' Harry didn't hear.

In her bedroom she opened the wall-length wardrobe. She ran her hand along the silks, velvets, seedy satins, cottons and crimplenes and sighed with pleasure. It was marvellous the upmarket gear you found if you went to the Double Bay op shop. Had to get there early, of course, or half the old Jewish Princesses would beat you to the draw. Never knew, as one said, if someone might not have thrown away a *classic* by mistake, darling. In fact, one had. Tried to get it back, too, darling, but that was another story. Sophie took out her bought-for-Balençiaga – simple line, floor-length, dark green silk and, with a lavish alteration to the hip, a more or less perfect fit.

'Great, Soph,' said Harry five minutes later, 'but what about your make-up?'

'Oh, Harr!' Sophie checked herself in the mirror.

'Go steady on the eye-liner,' advised Harry.

❖ ❖ ❖

The *Queen Elizabeth II* was moored at Circular Quay, near enough to the Opera House so that the geriatric passengers plated in platinum and diamonds could have a nice view of 'the concrete poem'.

Harry parked the car and they walked the last two hundred yards, Sophie regretting the high satin heels.

At the top of the gangway was a young talented smoothie with a bit of braid on his ducks. And Sophie definitely Junoesque and looking as if she were in the money. 'Good evening,' Sophie looked around: the direction was pretty clear. 'Why are we here, Harr?'

'Cultural and political junket. I'm representing the media.' Harry moved aside to let an elderly fat lady past.

Sophie took in the rich carpet and discreet lighting. 'She's huge – the boat, I mean.'

'She's two and a half football fields long,' Harry steered Sophie around the last corner.

'I'm not your bloody mother, Harry!' Sophie shook her arm free, checked her cigarettes were in her black evening bag, took one out and viewed the large stateroom. What looked like the Captain, in white and gold braid, but too old, was talking to a group of various Sydney notables while the geriatric passengers promenaded and smiled and picked at the caviar.

It was then that she noticed Charlie Dunn, or rather, Harry saw him and nudged her. One of Sophie's parlour tricks, after Charlie Dunn had risen to eminence in heart surgery, was an imitation of him operating on the Virgin Mary. Went down a treat as Charlie dragged out *Her* heart, found it flaming and dropped it, burning *his* fingers.

Sophie turned away from first cousin Charlie, the late Rosie's father, and made for the food. After a plate of oyster patties and a couple of crayfish tails in mornay sauce she would be ready to face anything.

Harry moved away to chat up a potential bedmate. Charlie Dunn made his way around a white-ducked officer. No point in pretending she hadn't seen him or darting into the banked greenery upstream.

Charlie Dunn had on his family smile but was not condescending. Charlie Dunn was in fact a little quivery about the lips. That was unusual, since Charlie Dunn belonged to the safe, secure Woollahra branch of the family, whose mother, Nell, had been a Parnell. Nell had turned to the Church of England, since that was the fate of Irish Catholics on the upwards turning wheel. She had recanted, of course, on her death bed, when heaven and hell were wheeling around her.

The Dunns were Anglo-Irish Protestant, which cousin Charlie never forgot, but old Nell's religious turn-about was hardly noticed, since Charlie didn't believe in anything that couldn't manifest itself in front of him. At the moment he was occupied with accepting Sophie's existence.

'I need to talk to you, Sophie,' said Charlie without further ado. 'How are your father and mother?' he asked as he steered her, older brother fashion, out on to the deck. Sophie looked again at the Harbour Bridge and the bright lights of Luna Park.

'Fine, Charlie.'

'It's about Rosemary, my daughter.' Charlie looked down at a ferry leaving for Balmain.

'I haven't met you since your mother died.' Sophie looked with him at the ferry. 'Nell's funeral. She had a requiem mass three days after she fell down the stairs. Remember, Charlie?'

'It was my Rosemary's inquest this afternoon. They delayed it for six months.'

'I'm sorry,' Sophie made a mental note to check on the newspaper report.

'We made sure nothing much got in the papers.'

'I'm sorry,' Sophie repeated.

'She was our youngest. Some people say she *jumped*.'

Sophie sat down and let herself take in Charlie Dunn. All around him was the aura of a request about to be made.

He was a big man, six feet tall, face lean and tanned, a strong jaw and clear ethnic Protestant eyes. He'd married, she remembered, in his third or fourth year of medical school. Now his hair was thinning and he was wearing one of those tailored suits in navy-blue that made the most of what line you've got left. He must have come straight from the inquest, Sophie thought.

It looked, too, as if Charlie Dunn had stopped off somewhere on the way and had a drink and a good cry.

'You've got to keep up appearances.' He grabbed at a passing tray of malt whiskies. 'Ruth couldn't manage it. She's at home, holding the fort. Worse really, for a woman,' Charlie drank down hard, 'so I came alone. I wasn't sure you'd be here, but it seemed as good a night as any to get on to you.' Charlie walked off and returned with another whisky and a plate of sandwiches. Sophie finished her mornay crayfish tails and took a fresh glass of wine.

'So you must be doing well. Hear good things about you. All that law training, I suppose. Fees must be OK.' Charlie checked out the Balençiaga.

12

Sophie lit a cigarette. Another ferry from North Sydney was waddling past the Queen, like an old nanny.

'I couldn't identify the remains; she'd been four months in the sea. Only the ring I gave her for her birthday. But that proved it, didn't it? I mean, even though the head was gone.'

Sophie supposed it did and tried to keep her mind off what Charlie must have looked down at on the marble slab.

'You see,' Charlie walked over to the rail and hung over it like a little boy, 'she was too young.' He straightened up again, face flushed. 'She was still a student at Sydney University. She travelled,' added Charlie vaguely, 'with her mate, Janet Craig, and a Thai bloke. Can't remember his name.'

'Where did she travel to?'

'Oh, Chiang Mai, and around.'

Chiang Mai, Sophie knew, was the place from where the pale-faced Thai girls were sent to the massage parlours in Bangkok, Asia's sex capital of the appropriate name.

Charlie fumbled for his wallet, found it, opened it and took out a photo to forget what he'd looked at on the mortuary slab. 'That was my Rosie, taken just ten days or so before she vanished.'

Sophie took the photo. Rosie had predictably blonde hair, soft lips curved in a Mona Lisa smile and high cheekbones. She looked like the kind of daughter Charlie would want. A good girl who would marry some professional boy and in the meantime stay on the pill.

'She had topaz eyes.' Charlie crumpled. 'They were strange eyes. It made her into something special, her eyes.'

'What was Rosie doing in Chiang Mai?' Sophie wanted to keep the conversation rolling. Charlie was from a world that didn't know weeping was now OK in public. Hadn't learned from Prime Minister Bob Hawke and assorted neophytes.

'Thesis.' Charlie appreciated Sophie's matter-of-fact tone. 'She was filling in time a bit. Something on the wedding rites of one of those tribes up there. Then it changed to the

13

status of women. Rosie said she was more likely to get a book out of it. She lost interest though. But they gave her a posthumous honours degree.'

'Was she up there often?'

'Three or four times.'

'What was the verdict at the inquest?'

'Open. She was seen leaving the Kings Cross flat she shared with Janet Craig, the girlfriend she travelled with. Two days later they found her things at the Gap.' Charlie took back the photo. 'The bloody Gap. Rosie wasn't the sort of girl to do that. She didn't have any reason.'

An image of the Gap came into Sophie's mind. She'd been young and romantic once, and had gone there, heart-broken, clasping Sylvia Plath's poems. She had taken a good long look at the giddying drop of hundreds of feet and the boiling surf around slabs of rock, then gone home and had a hot bath, several gins and T and a pepper steak dinner.

'I wonder which rock she went off?' Charlie put away his wallet. 'I mean, how far out did she jump? Did she close her eyes?'

'What do you think, Charlie?' Sophie made her voice intentionally hard and Charlie came to.

'I think she was thrown or pushed.'

'Why?' Sophie dusted down her silk handbag again. Some more wine had landed on it.

'Wrong company. Knew things.' He paused. 'I would like to kill *that* shit!'

Charlie stood up and began weaving towards the stairs. 'Let's go home and discuss. I've made up my mind. Let's go home and discuss details.'

Charlie Dunn was used to giving orders and Sophie remembered next month's mortgage payments. Harry was within cooee, still chatting up the easy-looking brunette. Sophie tipped him the nod and Harry looked pleased.

Sophie caught up with Charlie at the gangway as the young officer was assisting him to dry land. Charlie allowed, with a certain reserve that hinted at greater clout.

The silver-grey Mercedes Benz was parked close to the

wharf and Charlie ploughed towards it, as if he had the ball, was fighting off the opposing forwards and getting there. He opened the door, touched down and sat for a moment staring at the windscreen. His lips had a life of their own as Charlie Dunn wept again.

Sophie got in on her side. She offered a large handkerchief. Charlie Dunn took it and blew his nose.

'It's just that I loved her,' he said. He handed back the handkerchief and again was the forward struggling towards the goalposts. He switched on the ignition.

Sophie made a brief act of contrition as the Mercedes surged forward and found the turn into the city. She hoped the police weren't out with one of the booze buses. Charlie obviously couldn't have cared less. He had his alibi.

Sophie turned back to look at the flood-lit Queen as Charlie freewheeled up on to the Cahill Expressway, which would take them to the Eastern suburbs.

'I think,' said Sophie, 'it would be better if you came to my house, cousin Charlie.' She added as an afterthought, 'Since you're pissed.' She gave the address.

'Just direct me,' muttered Charlie.

They hurtled along in the fast lane, Charlie driving death away and still holding Rosie Dunn close, like a football against his chest, and them hurtling into the future like a meteor let loose on the world. Charlie Dunn was in the mood for vengeance.

Sophie tried to conjure up an image of Ruth Dunn, sitting at home by herself – weeping, she supposed, or going through her kid's clothes. Or staring at a wall, or getting stuck into the booze herself. Ruth had grey hair and was a solid sort of woman, they said. Not much given to emotion.

Charlie was first out of the car, looked at the number on the gatepost and got himself up the three steps and leaned against the ivied wall. Sophie followed, opened the door and led Charlie from the hall into the front room. There, the Brett Whiteley and the Norman Lindsay drawing showed a good front.

Charlie recognised the painting from the signature and

glanced around. 'I've got a Brett Whiteley too, in my rooms, of the Harbour Bridge. Bigger than yours,' said Charlie, 'but the bloody women like it.'

That decided Sophie, who wasn't going to show any signs of penis envy.

'OK,' Charlie spoke into the silence. 'It's my daughter we're talking about. You pay for that sort of thing.'

'In your world.' Sophie picked up Molly Meldrum, the jazz-loving marmalade tom.

'You see,' said Charlie Dunn, pulling out another photograph and staring at it, 'I think that Rufus Stone killed my Rosie and I think you'd be interested, since Rosie told me something about your brother David's death. It was murder too, in a way, wasn't it?'

He handed over the photograph. Sophie took it and the hackles on her neck went up. Rufus Stone and Rosie Dunn, together.

'Rosie knew that Rufus Stone was driving the car that killed David. She was staying with him, that weekend, up in Canberra. She told me just a few months before she was murdered.'

'But you didn't get on to me then, Charlie.'

Charlie had the grace to turn red. 'Too much scandal,' he mumbled, 'for Rosie.'

'But it's OK now that Rosie's dead?'

Charlie took the Black Label whisky and poured himself a small tot.

'I knew too, Charlie. It's how I got into private dickery. It's not the normal profession for a well-brought-up girl on the shelf, is it?'

'I thought that might have been the reason.' Charlie Dunn closed his eyes against a room that was starting to move around.

'David and Rufus Stone were at the same school,' said Sophie, forgetting her intentions to keep quiet and let him talk. 'Rufus was in the sixth form and David in the third. It was Branston, Charlie, except we came from North Sydney, and we began with the nuns. But then things changed.'

Branston! Sophie wearily closed her own eyes. Located in the Eastern suburbs it was the stamping ground for the male children of Sydney's more successful predators. The crown of Social Darwinism was a large Vaucluse house, a Mercedes and a son at Branston.

Some of them still believed with the social cringe set in that third-rate and sinking despotism, England, and Branston did its best to inculcate Britannic values. Which, under it all, were the same from Sydney to Boston – money and power, with a good surface manicure.

'Rufus Stone came from a short line of successful predators,' Sophie heard herself saying. 'Despite his name, which might have been Jewish, he was Irish. Bog like me, cousin Charlie, and like Nell, your mother. Not like the Dunns.'

'I know,' Charlie belched. 'Is that what you wrote in your logbook, Sophie?'

She fetched up Rufus Stone's face from her memory. Starting rich with his thick red hair and face like a Roman emperor, he got richer. One yacht, then two, two movie companies, then electronics, cattle stations, a couple of news-papers. But he made his real killing on the futures market – oil, cattle, gold. Then currency deals. Then boredom.

Boredom with women, too: women made and discarded, two failed marriages, the kids of one scattered about.

But by then he was beyond usual people and usual morality. He fed the pack but he never blended with them. Rufus Stone was a point of truth of which their run-of-the-mill manipulation, corruption – or ocker arrogance – was a weak reflection.

She turned to Charlie Dunn. 'Rufus knew the system through and through. Who to talk to, who to bribe, who to pay off. It was people like him who put me off law.'

'OK,' said Charlie Dunn, 'where's it all leading?'

'As you say, Rufus Stone killed my brother.' Her voice grew hard and Charlie Dunn reacted to it. His eyes opened and he looked at her again, almost sober.

'Sometimes I imagine the scene. The green Jaguar, an XK4, with Sydney numberplate, RUF 891. He was driving along

17

one of those roads near the Federal Parliament. You know, those roads that go nowhere since Canberra goes nowhere.'

'I don't like it either,' said Charlie.

'They say the car must have been going at least a hundred and sixty kilometres an hour. That would have been just enough speed to reduce David to mincemeat. I saw him, you see Charlie, just like you saw Rosie on *her* slab. Brother David had a little booze under his belt when he left his Embassy secretary at two in the morning.'

'Which Embassy?'

'French – exotic for Canberra. Anyone who can't speak English properly is a real find. Might be a mystery under those misplaced vowels.'

'Yeah,' said Charlie, grinning for the first time.

'He had had a good evening, so the doctor who performed the autopsy told me, as a kind of consolation prize,' Sophie continued.

'She'd been good to him, had she?' asked Charlie Dunn.

Sophie turned off the centre light and switched on the lamps.

'I tracked down the evidence, Charlie.' She paused and wondered whether to tell the rest. But it needed to be said, if Charlie and Ruth Dunn and their friends were to give up all they knew on Rosie, and on her friends and associates. It was better to square with Charles Dunn, the famous surgeon, she decided.

'I went to the Minister of Police, Charlie, who was in between scandals himself and taking a rest, so to speak, and when he refused action I threatened a news conference and a private prosecution.

'That way I would have got Rufus Stone, spread-eagled on the sand and just waiting for the vultures. I could almost see them flapping through the air, landing on a nearby tree and waiting to see who would be first to dig their beak in.'

Charlie looked at Sophie wryly. 'Hate to get on the wrong side of you,' he said.

'But it didn't happen, Charlie.

'That evening, you see, my father called me over for a

18

drink. We talked about business and he mentioned, en passant, what a good wake David had had and the Bishop visiting for the rosary, which had done Mum a power of good, not to mention the military guard of honour and the salute over the grave. And, he told me to leave the death alone!'

Sophie stared at the wall and then at a cicada that had found its way in. 'Dad cleared his throat and lit up a Drum roll-your-owns he'd been working on. He said "Leave it alone". It seemed someone had given him the word. I asked him who they were. Were they people like the Minister of Police, or one of his boozy priests, or Rufus Stone's friends? "People" was all he'd admit to. Then he said, "Rufus Stone must have forgotten to turn on the headlights. Or maybe he was drunk on the speed. I remember that when I was young. It was a motorbike and I got drunk on the speed. So maybe he didn't see David." I said to him, Charlie, "Maybe he saw him and put his foot down harder, like crushing a bug. Ever heard of snuff movies, Dad? They're made for businessmen who are bored!" But that was a stupid thing to say to him. It made it easier for him. Dad, you see, believes in decent men who look after each other and don't make waves. At heart, cousin Charlie, he's quite like you. Quite like a lot of decent men.'

Sophie picked the cicada off the wall and liberated it out the window. She was in full flow – inside – the cosmic soprano winging her way through the ethical and spiritual realms. The aria moving towards its necessary conclusion! 'Then he said,' Sophie turned to observe Charlie, ' "No good can come from putting yourself against Rufus Stone, Sophie. You'll lose your clients as well. No one will touch anyone who touches Rufus Stone and it won't bring my boy back." '

'So Terence retired then, did he?' asked Charlie. 'Too much for him?'

'Yes, up to Surfer's Paradise. It was a condominium and they bought a penthouse. Mum told me it cost around two hundred and fifty thousand dollars. It is luxury, Charlie. You know, a swimming-pool, and a golf course near by.'

She waited for a moment. 'I checked on the company. It was a subsidiary of Rufus Stone's.

'So I left David's death alone since we had been paid off. In fact, from Rufus Stone's point of view we'd done quite well. And that was because people who knew had respect for the Parnells and their place in the world and paid out blood money.'

Charlie stared at Sophie, then brought out his cheque book. 'How much would you be asking?' was all he said.

Sophie came back to herself with a start. 'Twenty thousand dollars, Charlie. Plus expenses. And they include whatever and whoever I think needs to be bought or paid for. I'll bill you once a month. You pay half the fee now and half on completion.'

'I'll double the fee.' Charlie Dunn began writing. 'Rose, my Rose, had a life insurance policy and it reverted back to me. It should be used to find out why she lost her life.'

He handed her the cheque. 'But I can't afford personal scandal, and I can't afford threats against myself or my wife and kids. So if you take it, you have to think up your own alibi. Why you're doing it on your own behalf.'

'You're clever, Charlie.'

'You've written some journalistic stuff on Sydney scandals. Pretend you're doing a story. Or a book.' Charlie was warming up. 'You could be doing a book on drugs and corruption in Sydney, and that doesn't mean you're after Rufus Stone in particular. But I'll know you are. Rosie told me he'd moved into drug finance.'

A set look came across his face. 'I remember something Rosie said about him. That he was tough, even brutal sometimes. She said no one crossed him. She said that she might cross him, one day, with what she knew.'

'So, I'll write a book.'

'As an excuse, Sophie. But it won't really be written. The Dunns don't like that sort of publicity.' Charlie began to play with his silk tie. His hands had the practised taut gentleness of someone used to the scalpel. 'I think Ruth had better be your contact. It's easy for you women to meet shopping, up the street maybe, or at the Saturday market at Paddington. I'll give her Rosie's diary. It's a pocketbook one. I found it in one of her coats.'

'Tell Ruth to be up at the market tomorrow at ten thirty,' said Sophie. 'Tell her to bring whatever photos you have of Rufus Stone and Rosie together, one of Rosie alone, any letters over the last two years.'

She glanced at the cheque on the coffee table. 'You want to know what happened to Rosie Dunn?'

Charlie nodded.

'You're quite certain?' Sophie felt again that peculiar lightness that came over her when she knew whatever would happen would reach a successful conclusion.

Charlie nodded again. 'That's your job. You're being paid for it.'

'Yes, Charlie, I just hope that for you it will be worth it.'

'You've got that Celtic thing, haven't you?' Charlie stared at her.

'Yes, Charlie. Just sometimes.'

Charlie ambled to the door. 'I don't believe in second sight.'

'One more thing, Charlie. Who tipped you off I'd be at the reception?'

Charlie adjusted his jacket. 'Your friend Harry. I saw him a couple of days ago and checked you out. He's looking for investors in a film. Ruth likes the idea and the tax cover is good. He said he was taking you tonight, and somehow it all fitted together.'

'More than you know, Charlie. I finished a case today.'

Charlie looked at Sophie again, but the fey look had vanished.

He opened the front door and got himself down the steps more by guess than sight. He climbed into the silver-grey Mercedes and reversed out. With a clash again of gears the car turned and Charlie Dunn drove away, seated upright like any soldier looking in the right direction, every inch what life had made of him.

3

Ruth had rung the next morning, voice quavery. She claimed a bout of the flu but didn't bother turning on a fit of coughing. Sophie guessed the relationship with Ruth Dunn wouldn't run smooth. Sophie offered condolences. Ruth replied, distant in her self, as if viewing Rosie's death and her flu from some other plane. Sudden arctic pauses developed as Ruth struggled for courtesy. The appointment was put off until the following Saturday.

It suited Sophie well enough. It gave her time to hand in the report on Jamey boy and accept, with sweaty palms, the last small cheque for her services to the State.

Jamey boy had been down at the Darlinghurst police station with the Fraud Squad most of the weekend. He had been grilled, but no boots in the belly or sudden trippings down concrete stairs.

Sophie herself had been in on Monday and was treated with wary courtesy. After that she'd checked the findings of the Dunn inquest. Evidence had been given by Janet Craig, described as unemployed, address 40 Victoria Street, Kings Cross. Janet Craig had apparently missed Rosie after forty-eight hours. She'd rung the Dunns, who'd come down. Together they'd made a police report. At the same time the bag and shoes were found at the Gap.

Other people came forward to attest Rosie was/had been a student. Her thesis was mentioned, as was the posthumous honours degree offered at the last degree ceremony.

Then the 'open' verdict. No reasons for suicide, no evidence of foul play. The case was open as far as the Court was concerned. Open but closed. It was the kind of thing you would expect.

Whatever Rosie Dunn had been, she was now gone and violets would grow over her grave. Except the Dunns were modern and hygenic. Rosie's ashes, so Ruth Dunn had told Sophie in her second phone call, would be scattered from a boat at Camp Cove, in the calm harbour waters. It would be preceded by a memorial service at the Woollahra Anglican Church. Sophie had made note of the date – Tuesday week. Ruth had also reconfirmed the meeting for that Saturday at the market.

It was Janet Craig, however, who was Sophie's chief interest. Janet Craig was not unemployed. Janet Craig was, Sophie now knew, a hooker. Had been for around a year, according to contacts at the Cross. She'd got Jamey boy to ask some questions about her. Didn't want her own name circulating before she had a chance to interview the lady.

'Real easy, Sophie.' Jamey had lit up a cigarette and looked more relaxed than she'd ever seen him before. 'She's considered kinda high class. Speaks with a posh accent.'

'So she should.' Sophie put down her capuccino. 'She went to my school.'

'Turns out a load of slack tarts these days,' said Jamey.

'Chamfield girls have always been noted for their enterprise.' Sophie's austere tone surprised Jamey.

They left the Kings Cross Brasserie and walked for a while through the streets.

'Any news of the trial date?' Sophie arrived at her Volkswagon. Jamey put his hands in his pockets. 'Not yet. They reckon it could be six months, but Michael, my Dad, is going to see if it can be put up on the list. Get it over and done with.' Sophie handed Jamey thirty dollars.

Jamey slipped it into his shirt pocket. 'That friend of yours, Harry Bowers, reckons he can get me something on a film.'

'Which film?' Sophie turned on the ignition.

23

'Something about the old gangster days in Sydney.'

'Should be right up your street, Jamey boy. What doing?'

'Assistant gaffer.' Jamey bent down to the open window and gave Sophie a kiss on her cheek. 'Thanks a million, Soph.'

That was Wednesday afternoon.

Today was Saturday and the alarm was ringing. Sophie opened her eyes. Still not a word from Cliffie. The longest sulk he'd had. She glanced at the photo of brother David on the bedside table. One she'd taken herself when she bought the Leica. David had had red hair and a pale skin that never tanned properly. He was grinning.

Sophie left the house at ten twenty and wandered up to the Paddington Market, three minutes away.

On the footpath the punks and Boy Georges were sunning themselves in seeming androgynous promiscuity. A group of Columbians were singing about space and mountains and were all smiles. It was that kind of weather. Sunny, but a cold snap in the air. Sophie added twenty cents to the guitar case, already filling up.

In the walk-through, the white tubs were crammed full of flowering petunias. Beside them Ruth was sitting on a low brick wall behind an amateur tarot card reader. Ruth was wearing a twinset and brown skirt, and seemed uncomfortable. She was holding a leash. At the end of it was a Corgi who looked as if he mostly got about by car.

Apart from being out of her territory, there was a stiffness about Ruth's back and her face that reminded Sophie of an old nun she'd been taught by. It was a face given to judgement. That broke when Ruth saw her. It was not exactly a thaw, but the lips half formed a smile, and Sophie knew Ruth Dunn was a frightened woman who'd been testing her strength to herself.

Sophie sat down beside her and Ruth, with her greying blonde hair, nodded. 'I'm a bit under the weather still. Charlie's been difficult too. It's as if Rosie,' she could hardly say the name, 'is finally dead for him.' Ruth paused.

'Rosie was Charlie's favourite.' She moistened her lips. 'Had it been Heather or Tom I don't think he would have . . .

would have employed a . . . employed you.' Ruth reached down to the bag by her feet.

'Not yet, Ruth.' Sophie took off her sunglasses as Ruth put hers on. 'What have you got for me?'

'Some letters from Rosie when she was in Thailand. A photo of Rosie taken just before she – died. A photo of Rosie and Rufus Stone, and one of Mr Stone by himself. On a raft. There is also one of a Thai boy. I think he was, for a time, Rosie's friend.'

Ruth looked around the market.

'What sort of a girl was Rosie Dunn?'

Ruth had been expecting that question; had obviously been thinking about it. Her lips compressed. 'Rosie was a very innocent girl, in her own way. I used to think she was fey, something genetic she got from her grandmother, Nell. Mind, she was an affectionate, a loving girl. She and Charlie were very close.' Ruth dabbed her lips.

'Did she change after Thailand?'

Ruth Dunn looked at the tarot reader laying out the Celtic Cross. 'Yes, she changed. She was less interested in her studies. Also, she was having a *relationship* of which I did not approve. Girls of Rosie's age should keep to young fellows. I felt it wasn't natural – the relationship.'

'Rufus Stone?' Sophie glanced at the Celtic Cross. Someone was coming in for good luck according to the tarot reader whose hair needed a wash and possible delousing.

Ruth nodded. 'Mr Stone is a very important man. He has a lot of power and a lot of influence. I told Rosie she should not expect anything lasting. That the glamour might not do her any good. But Rosie always decided herself what she would do. Not that she didn't listen and consider, but we brought them all up to make up their own minds.'

'And hers was to be with Rufus Stone?'

Ruth Dunn tugged on the Corgi's lead.

'And was it also her decision to dob Rufus Stone in?'

'We have done nothing but talk of it. There is, simply, no rational reason for Charles's view. No rational reason at all to think that Mr Stone has drug interests. But then, they say, fathers can be a little irrational when it comes to their daughters. We have *no* evidence that Rufus Stone did harm.'

Ruth was beginning to fray at the edges like a Dallas soapy queen.

'What about Rosie's knowledge of my brother David's death? That was Rufus Stone. It takes a great deal of intimacy to tell someone that. You don't tell a casual lay that you've committed manslaughter and concealed it. An official cover-up. That would not do Rufus Stone good if it got out. Wouldn't do the police and politicians involved good, either. Wake up, Ruth. In this day and age in New South Wales contracts have been put out for less.'

Ruth bent down and patted the Corgi, called him 'Roger' like a favoured child. Roger licked her hand.

'Was Rosie Dunn just his casual lay, Ruth?'

Ruth's hand was shaking.

'No, she couldn't have been. I didn't know – about David. I'm sorry. It is just, all, all so wicked. Charlie never told me. Never mentioned it.'

'But *who* has caused the wickedness, Ruth?'

Ruth's eyes were bleak. 'A ghost is causing this, isn't it? A ghost and Charlie Dunn.'

'You don't want this investigation, do you?'

Ruth reached into her bag and brought out a fat envelope. 'This is everything I could find on Rosie.'

'I'll want to talk to your other children.'

'They know nothing.' Ruth Dunn stood up. 'You will *not* trouble them. I am hoping that this, this investigation, will soon peter out. Children cannot understand how wicked this world can be. They must be protected, Sophie, from publicity. From all of this. Rosie would want it so.'

'Really, Ruth?' Sophie also stood up – and could think of no way of putting it gently. 'You know Rosie was living with Janet Craig. You also know Janet Craig pays for her rent by whoring. Janet Craig has become a hooker, Ruth, and Rosie must have been living with her when Janet became a hooker. I want you to ring Janet, and tell her I'll be visiting.'

Ruth picked up her bag. 'I have things to do,' she told Roger, 'some shopping for Charlie. He needs new underpants.'

'I want to interview Janet Craig, Ruth, and perhaps other people you know.'

Ruth nodded and took off her sunglasses. 'Charlie has asked me to be the go-between. I agreed to do that. More than that, I won't do.' She tucked her bag under her arm. 'Rosie was my last child. I had her at thirty-six. Now I'm sixty and Charlie is fifty-two. Male menopause, I suppose. I was older than him, you see, and I had a private income.'

She strode away with the Corgi, a slightly mannish figure, straight of back, to continue living out whatever she and Charlie Dunn had made of life.

Perhaps she was right about Charlie Dunn, thought Sophie. Male menopause. The child dying. First, resisting the idea, then looking for someone to blame. The guilt. Ruth had guilt, there was no doubt of that. Guilt and fear.

Sophie put the thick envelope into her shoulder bag and wandered into the bustle of Paddington Market. She bought some incense sticks and felt another twinge for Cliffie.

Marjorie, Charlie's former sister-in-law, was waiting for her in the church hall, as arranged. Sophie bought a couple of fresh carrot juices and carried them over to where she was sitting.

Marjorie had recently found herself a job, a new man and a smaller house. She and Sophie had always kept up. More so since Marjorie had divorced Thomas, Charlie's boring brother.

'So what have you dug up?'

Marjorie took her carrot juice. 'My daughter Karen was a great friend of Rosie's, a while back.'

'And?' Sophie took in Marjorie's honest face. Something in her like a border sheepdog.

'They drifted apart when Rosie went to uni. Karen went into the gem business with her father. Then Rosie came into the office around November. Not last November, she was dead by then.' Majorie's warm voice faltered for a moment.

'Go on.'

'She wanted a ring, and an unofficial deal. You know, you give your address in Paris and no tax. Karen cooked the books for her. It was an emerald, an Australian emerald. A beauty, Karen said. It came from one of those desert mines. Up north somewhere.'

'How much?'

'With forty per cent discount, ten thousand dollars.'

Sophie finished her carrot juice.

'It's a lot of money, Sophie, for a girl of twenty-three to fork out.'

'Did she?'

Marjorie shook her head.

'Karen said the signature on the cheque was Rufus Stone's.' She paused again. 'Why would he do that, Sophie. I mean, I heard they had a thing, but ten thousand dollars?'

'Rufus Stone will answer that for me.' Sophie squeezed Marjorie's hand. 'One day he will. One day soon.'

'Charlie thinks Rufus Stone did her in.' Marjorie picked up her parcels.

'What was Rosie like?' asked Sophie.

'Like any other kid. Bit self-righteous over causes, but she lost that I gather. When she first went up to Chiang Mai she was scandalised at how little the growers were making out of opium. I mean,' Marjorie started her dry laugh, 'didn't she think of what *heroin* does to people. I mean, what does it *matter* what the growers are paid!!'

They moved out into the market. Marjorie stopped at a stall selling ponchos and ruyanas. 'The real truth is she was just a niece. Family don't bother telling you who they are. They're really just part of the jigsaw pattern. It's only when they've gone you look at the empty space and wonder.'

'So what do you wonder?'

Marjorie selected a brown alpaca ruyana and bought it with a crisp new fifty-dollar note. 'She was too young, only twenty-three or so. It's not until thirty that people are formed. You know, after they've suffered a bit.'

'Did Rosie suffer?'

Marjorie shook her head. 'Rosie wasn't capable yet of

suffering. It didn't exist for her. Karen thought she was great, when they were younger. She said Rosie could get right inside you and become you. She said Rosie empathised with her. That was a big word for Karen then, "Empathy".' Marjorie let out some smoke in a splutter of laughter then coughed a dry smoker's cough. 'Whatever that was.'

They reached the pavement. 'I'm not surprised at Charlie. He pays you, and you take the rap if it comes. If you'd not been family Charlie would never have acted. Now it's in the family, and if anyone pays, you do, an unmarried cousin, regarded as a bit disreputable anyway. He's clever, Sophie. If I were you I'd give him back his cheque and forget about it.'

'So what did you come up with? You know, the empty space in the jigsaw puzzle that Rosie Dunn left?'

'I suppose that I didn't like her. Never had really. Too good, too understanding, and those bloody eyes. Always watching other people.'

They kissed, and Marjorie wandered off down the street to where her red Renault was parked.

Sophie hadn't been inclined to mention the size of Charlie's cheque. Though she trusted Marjorie, even well-intentioned people couldn't resist an indiscretion on occasions after a few glasses of wine. Nor did she want to say that it had paid off her mortgage while the twenty to come would do up the rest of the house and provide a holiday in New York. Prosaic details that Marjorie, well-off after the divorce, had long forgotten about. Her settlement, so the rumours went, had not only been substantial but, even stranger, amicable.

Sophie sat and listened for a while to the South Americans. Put in a dollar and was rewarded with a flashing smile. She strolled further and watched the conjurer who had collected a gaggle of kids, then she walked home.

4

Janet Craig lived in Victoria Street at Kings Cross. Number 40 was one of those old terraced buildings with a wooden top-floor verandah that hosted a large number of olive-green leaved plants.

Sophie brooded with them for a moment before noticing a discreet card. Janet Craig was on the top floor. The hall door was open. There were wine stains on the sea-grass matting.

She faced Janet's door from a short-order landing. One window offered light and the view of a small garden – stalky geraniums, a bougainvillea growing up against the rotten slats of a fence. Beyond was a lane where a spotty-faced youth was shooting up. Beside the window were two posters. The first of almost-Senator Peter Garrett of Midnight Oil. He'd stood on the Nuclear Disarmament ticket in the Federal elections but lost out on a seat since Labor, in the complex distribution process, had given their preferences to their main rivals, the Liberals. Labor out of office had ethics but in office had found themselves with a born-again power broker, Bob Hawke of late and lamented honour. One of those lapsed Calvinists that Protestantism spawns and capitalism nourishes, thought Sophie with a burst of her old radical spite.

The Bob Hawke poster had a few rude comments scrawled across his nose and cheeks. Sophie was tempted to add her own, then remembered her age and profession.

Janet Craig wouldn't have a customer around lunch time. According to Jamey, they came in the evening or for late-night appointments.

Sophie rang the bell.

Footsteps sounded inside. Sophie was checked out through the spy hole. The door was opened.

'Hallo.'

Janet Craig had black hair cut square and a square face.

She had obviously just got out of bed, and the mascara under her eyes was smudged. She still had a good figure from those days at Chamfield when a young lady went over the long horse, touched her toes and swam ten lengths of the pool every day. She was wearing a yellow silk dressing-gown, which was somehow incongruous. Or was it because of her job? Janet Craig was built for sensible clothes, a sheep station kitchen and kids, a horse and a pilot's licence. But here she was, a whore.

'I'm Sophie Parnell.' Sophie gave a warm maternal smile. 'I wonder if I could talk to you. Ruth Dunn said she'd call you.'

Janet Craig evidently remembered all the amenities of middle-class living.

'Yes, of course,' she said politely.

Sophie got herself across the threshold before a sudden flicker of suspicion could bring on second thoughts. But Janet was still concentrating on good manners. 'I'm making a cup of coffee, would you like one?' She disappeared.

It was a comfortable room, painted cream with some framed posters: one of Toulouse Lautrec and one from the Sydney Picasso exhibition. There was a signed Dali lithograph. Close by it was a small pine bookcase. Sophie wandered over to it. The titles were what one would expect from a Chamfield girl with any brains she had kept well in check.

Sophie padded into the kitchen. Beyond, in a glassed-in verandah among spider plants falling from their wire baskets, stood Janet Craig. Her face was concentrated on the plunger of a needle. She was pressing down slowly into a bulging vein in her elbow. Beside her, on a wooden bench, was her equipment.

Gradually, her face lost its concentration and she stood there in the golden light, slowly releasing the rubber cord. *Hail Thou That art Highly favoured, the Lord is with thee. Blessed art thou amongst women and Blessed be the fruit of thy womb* . . .

Janet smiled slowly. It rippled across her face as if she were enjoying some delicious secret. She pulled out the needle and applied some cotton wool. 'Yeah. Well,' was all she said.

They walked back into the sitting room.

'So you want to know about Rosie Dunn. Do *they* all know?' Janet lit a cigarette slowly and slowly inhaled.

Sophie shook her head. 'Only Charlie and Ruth, and she's not interested in any investigation.'

'Par for the course.' Janet took another puff. In the kitchen the coffee on the gas ring began to perk. Down by Sophie's feet was her Peruvian shopping basket. Inside, the tape in the cassette would be moving.

'What sort of a woman was Rosie Dunn?'

'She always wanted to go into business,' said Janet unexpectedly. 'That is, before she met Rufus Stone. We thought we might open a boutique on Oxford Street. Something like *Rosie Nice*. You know, upmarket and good cuts to the clothes. Good fabrics, too. We thought we'd go over to Italy and France and buy samples.'

'And then?'

'She didn't like being called Rosie, either. Her mother was the one who called her that and Tom and Heather followed suit, but she liked Rose because it reminded her of the flower. Sweet smelling! I used to laugh and say most of the modern sort smelled like plastic nothings. Real rip-offs. Rose would say they looked the part and that was what counted. And besides, her father called her Rose when they were alone together. It was his special name for her.'

Janet Craig was floating somewhere else.

'My play is that I'm doing a book. It's the way Charlie wanted it, with Rosie as a possible case study. Maybe a victim?'

Janet Craig again smiled a deep inwards smile and again looked like a Madonna communing with her destiny.

'We were up in Chiang Mai four times. We were both

supposed to be researching our theses. Then Rosie met a man.'

'The Thai boyfriend?'

'So you know about him?' Janet went to fetch the coffee. 'We found out some interesting stuff through Luk. Some of it, in laundered form, could have been used for our theses, although, by then I'd given up on the idea. We started ingesting opium, but it only made Rosie sick. She didn't like smoking heroin either. Luk got me on to that. They call it Angel's Breath. It was for me, but it gave Rosie vile hallucinations.'

'What other interesting things did you find out?'

Janet lay back and closed her eyes. 'Ruth said you'd call. She also asked me not to see you. She said you were an interfering busybody but by law she couldn't stop you. Nothing about Charlie paying you. She also said she thought you were probably a dyke. She said no normal woman would do what you do.'

Sophie forced herself to keep her mouth shut.

'Ruth Dunn said that, alive and dead, Rosie attracted unfortunate people. That was Ruth's little kick at me. I told her I would see you. I also told her Rosie Dunn and I had had, how do they call it in French, a *ballade*?' Janet half finished the cup. 'I said I would be happy to see a dyke any day of the week, since I was one, too.'

'Then you'll co-operate?'

'Oh, yes.' Janet lay back again.

'Then start at the beginning.'

Janet put down her cup. 'It started when we went to Grace's Bar in Bangkok. Rosie and I wanted to see one of the joints and Luk knew the owner. Otherwise, for two blondes – my hair was dyed in those days – it might have been dangerous.

'Grace's Bar is under a posh hotel. There were lots of girls sitting at tables and lots of men at the bar, mostly Aussies with a few French and Germans. The girls would try to get a male to sit down with them, grope a bit and hope for an erection. None of your sophisticated, *noli me tangere*.'

'Latin at Chamfield?' asked Sophie.

'The air was thick with sweat and smoke and perfume,' said Janet, back in her past and still free-floating. 'All the girls made up. Very elegant and very tasteful. The music was loud and the old Chinaman who runs it grinning like hell. He had reason. He took a small cut from the girls who made a client and the beers flowed. There were a few fans but they only stirred up the gunk.

'Then a European came in with a very attractive older Thai woman. Some girls made way at a good table and they sat down. No one joined them, but now and then a girl would come up and sometimes would be invited to sit down. They never stayed for more than ten minutes or so. Luk was a bit pissed. He'd made some business deal and the deal had paid off well. Rosie asked him who they were. He grinned and said it was a very successful partnership we were watching.'

Janet paused. 'Maybe if she hadn't asked, nothing would ever have happened. Rosie might still be alive.'

'Who was it?' Sophie took in Janet Craig's face. For a moment something that looked like pain showed itself.

'A guy called Jim Stokes. In the consular section of the Oz Embassy. What he did was supply visas, for three thousand to five thousand bucks. The girls got a student visa. They enrolled at one of the universities and someone took their place for exams. After two or three years they'd made a lot of money.'

'Surely not enough to pay back that amount?'

'Oh yes, on Oz wages. And then there's the other scam. Those that can't pay it all act as couriers for the drug network. They deal, they hold the stuff. Some of them supplement with prostitution. Others work in restaurants. They usually get enough cash together to go back home, buy into partnership as a Mama San of a small establishment or even find a husband. Some of them marry in Australia and stay on.'

'And that was Jim Stokes' scam?'

Janet nodded. 'That and drugs. Jim Stokes was an agent for the Australian connection. He's back here now, working out of the State Attorney's Office. He's supposed to be investigating Thai/Oz drug link-ups.' Janet laughed dryly. 'Some cover, isn't it?'

The room had suddenly got cold. Sophie switched on the fan heater. She glanced down at her coffee, three-quarters undrunk.

Janet Craig went to the drinks tray. 'What will it be?'

'A small whisky. Don't worry about ice. No water.'

Janet poured herself a dry sherry.

'Do the Dunns know about all this?'

Janet shook her head. She sat down again.

'Then Luk went over to their table and it seems business was over and Jim Stokes joined us. He took an immediate shine to Rosie. Most men did.'

'Didn't you feel it?'

Janet gave her a look as one dyke to another. 'Why don't we go to lunch, down at the Opera House.'

Janet went out of the room.

'What time's your first customer?'

'Customer?' Janet called back from the bedroom. 'At four. An advertising executive. He'd probably like your type. You know, the matronly bit. He's an advertising executive from Adelaide. Pays on his credit card. He'll be eating a long lunch, oiling himself up on wine and fantasising about how virile he is. He thinks I'm in love with him and I'll be cheerful and bustling. He really wants a girlfriend who understands him. Christ!' Janet reappeared in baggy trousers and a bright checked shirt. 'He talks about Betty, his wife, whose a real bitch, into money and booze and half the Golf Club. He's a regular, most of them are.'

She picked up her shoulder bag. 'All you need is a bit of method acting and a little of what Rosie had. You know, empathy. Climb into their fantasies and live them for them.'

❖ 5 ❖

They sat at the prow of the Opera House. Olive trees in white wooden casks framed the water, the billowing spinnakers, stretches and inlets, the rich luxury of sea-held Sydney. Janet Craig had ordered a chicken curry then left to make a phone call. Sophie had ordered the same. Janet and the food arrived at the same moment. The view, thought Sophie, was presumably the sauce that excused the chef.

Janet Craig ate sparingly. She sipped her wine.

'Rosie's downfall started with Luk. She used to call him "Good". At first it was just a fling and then it became a kind of love. You know, since you don't understand the person or their culture, they become romantic?

'Luk came down here and Rosie bought her apartment. Luk used it at first for his dealing. Rosie acted as courier. I got on the game to pay for my stuff. Luk found me customers and some of Jim Stokes' contacts came good.

'Then Luk went back to Thailand and Rosie realised she didn't really love him. He was on to his own thing. He was married too. Rosie laughed a bit at herself and laughed a bit anyway. She'd kept records of the meetings and the people. A few politicians, a few policemen and some of Jim Stokes' associates. She knew drop places, entry points, and a lot more. It was the habit she'd continued from her thesis. She told me then that she thought Rufus Stone was one of the big financiers behind it all.' Janet Craig smiled as if receiving her death sentence. 'She had evidence on him within a year.'

Sophie felt herself beginning to sweat and moved into the shade of the overhead umbrella.

'That came when we went up to Chiang Mai again. We'd decided to take a holiday on a raft with Jim Stokes. He appeared with Rufus Stone, both dressed in white I remember, like colonial planters. We all had dinner together that night. Rosie was fascinated by Rufus. He has a kind of aura of sex and power. He's also amusing and you can feel under it something like a buccaneer. Not the romantic type but the real thing. One of those Companions of Fortune.

'Most men like him don't go anywhere near Thailand. They sit in their fortieth-storey offices and collect the money, but he couldn't resist finding out what it was really all about.

'Rosie and he talked, and Rufus started to take an interest in her. It was as if he was meeting a protégée. He decided to come on the trip too.

'They were great, the rafts. Rufus and Jim had one to themselves and Rosie and I were on the other. Rufus arranged that. He didn't want more company than necessary. The crew were locals and two of them cooked. Sometimes we'd run aground and have to get out and push.

'Then it happened and Rosie shifted on to Rufus' raft and Jim to mine. We floated down between the banks, heavy jungle in some parts. In the evenings we moored and Rufus and Chiang Mai Bill, as Rosie called the number one cook, would throw in some sticks of dynamite down river. After the explosions we'd wade in and collect the fish. What we couldn't eat Chiang Mai Bill would sell at one of the villages.

'Around five thirty we'd drink Mekong whisky, and sometimes I and Jim Stokes joined Rufus and Rose for dinner. But it was by royal invitation. You didn't venture on to Imperial territory unless Rufus Stone wanted it.

'At the second last stop Rufus had arranged a surprise. He'd had champagne flown up from Bangkok and he had a party at a local restaurant, on the river. It was to show off Rosie. He'd known what would happen. He'd also ordered her a necklace and bracelets. They were in silver and golden sapphires. The local military governor came with some of his henchmen and a few Europeans and a few Chinese.

'Rosie was the hostess and the men's eyes were on her. She was dressed in white, and the yellow sapphires were almost the colour of sunset. And her eyes! That wonderful topaz shade! She looked extraordinary!

'Rufus Stone thought so too, and that night they left. When they got back, a week later, Rosie had changed. She told me she would stay with Rufus Stone. And she did. She was often in Canberra at his house. And sometimes in Sydney. But she kept it quiet. She never wanted anything public. I think it was more exciting that way.'

'Then why did Rufus Stone have her murdered?'

Janet picked up the bill and waved to the waitress. She took out her credit card. An American Express Gold.

They wandered off down the walkway. Janet stopped and looked out over the harbour.

'She fought with Rufus Stone. He bashed her around. That had never happened to Rosie before. You see, after a while she had started dealing on the sly, and that threatened Rufus. He told her where she stood.

'So when she came back that day before she vanished, it was as if she was the Rosie Dunn Charlie and Ruth had always wanted. She was trembling, but it wasn't just with cold. She told me she had all the information she needed. You see, being hit by a man had made Rosie Dunn grow up.' Janet looked at the water. 'She became Charlie Dunn's daughter for the first time, and a Chamfield girl. A respectable girl. A girl who couldn't be touched, couldn't be thrown across a bed and beaten by a man's fists and then fucked into obedience.

'I remember it was raining that day and she had on a yellow mac. She was soaking, but I couldn't get it off her.

'So she went home to Charlie Dunn.

'Ruth was away at the Palm Beach house and Rosie knew Charlie wouldn't notice the way Ruth would. She told him she'd split her lip falling down the stairs and he sewed it up for her.

'Then she sat and thought about things and decided to take the knife to Rufus Stone. She never believed, you see, that what happened to drug addicts, to poor girls, could happen to her. Had she understood, she would have kept the papers safe, somewhere, as a protection, as a defensive weapon.

'I went out after it was in the papers. Into the Cross. Walked for hours until dawn. You know how it is, the real Cross. Vomit on the pavements, syringes, the deros sleeping and paper blowing about. Mostly paper blowing about.'

'Who did it?'

Janet ignored the question.

'She did, however, make a copy of the papers, the names, the people, the drop points, sometimes the conversations she was in on. She gave some of the stuff to me. I read it through and . . .'

'Destroyed it?' Sophie was watching a busker dressed in tattered Indian trousers and a shirt. He was playing 'Hey Mr Tambourine Man, Play a Song for Me'. 'You destroyed it!'

'No.' Janet threw away her cigarette and looked at a ferry coming in from Manly. 'No, I kept it. But it doesn't incriminate Rufus Stone. It gets as far as Jim Stokes. He's the front man for Rufus Stone. Rosie said there was more. But what she left with me was the copy of the stuff that led to Jim Stokes.'

'Who did she go to?'

'She made an appointment with the Drug Squad and she handed in the stuff. And then, the next day, she vanished.'

They had almost reached the end of the Opera Plaza. Coming towards them was a woman, tall, slender, wearing dark wraparound sunglasses. She stopped when she saw Janet.

'Hello, Janet.'

There was a trace of American overlaid on the Australian accent.

Janet made the introductions. 'This is Sophie Parnell, Elise. Elise Cadogan, Sophie Parnell.'

Elise Cadogan looked briefly at Sophie but her face remained expressionless. Sophie felt momentarily disconcerted. Elise Cadogan seemed to find her a specimen to be studied. 'Nice to meet you,' she finally said.

Sophie smiled.

'It's a great day for walking,' Elise Cadogan smoothed back her hair. 'No other city in the world can offer this.' She gestured at the harbour. 'See you.' She walked on.

'See you,' called out Janet.

'Film star material,' commented Sophie.

❖ ❖ ❖

Sophie stood in Janet Craig's bedroom while she knelt in front of the fireplace and reached up into the chimney. She looked up at Sophie. 'It's still there.'

She withdrew a package.

'Here,' she said, 'take it. I've read it all. I read it after she gave it to me. Then I put it up there. God,' she smoothed down her hair, 'all that time ago.'

Sophie took it.

It was only when she was back in her car that she realised her hands, which should have been soot covered, were clean.

◆ 6 ◆

Branston wasn't on the way home but it wasn't much further along New South Head Road.

The school of weathered mellow sandstone stood by itself, high on a hill overlooking the harbour waters. The goal posts had been put up for the football season. In the quad the school was on parade. Cadet day or week. Anyway, a lifetime's occupation. Among them would be David's ghost, making the smart right turn, the smart salute and smart about turn.

Sophie parked the car and wandered along the wide tree-lined drive. Somewhere, *there*, would be the new science block under construction to be named the Rufus Stone block. One day, perhaps, an oil painting, too, in the foyer, with Rufus in a suitably heroic pose. She passed a few boys dressed in their black and white striped blazers. She made her enquiries and was told the upper school were on parade for some mass misdemeanour.

She lost the impetus to re-explore and returned to her car.

The Gap was ten minutes further on and she could feel its presence before reaching it. Like a magnet, a power centre for Sydney's negations and pretences, the cleansing leap, the convenient disposal of unwanted souls. The sandstone cliffs in brown and maroon had the same mellow texture and colour as Branston. The stone, for all she knew, might have been quarried from this spot.

A southerly had got up and with it the chill of a distant-approaching autumn. She pulled on an old cardigan and stepped out and over the low fence.

There was the path, carefully trodden down to make the approach to the edge easier. It was too easy, not penitential enough. Too easy for those who had come here one dark winter's night of last August and had dragged a drugged or dead Rosie Dunn along.

Sophie arrived at the edge, and the waves below were as they would have been then, white and grey and winter flecked. Great surging, gutting movements of water.

Certainly Rosie Dunn hadn't walked here, calm and certain, consumed by her fate. She hadn't walked over to that ledge which would carry her clear into the waves. No! She would have been thrown from some convenient place around the turn of the tide, which had been at one in the morning. That would carry her out to where she would catch an ocean current. The one that had caught her and pulled her northwards towards the tropics and deposited her in a fishing net just one hundred kilometres from here.

The fisherman had vomited when he saw what he had caught and what he must disentangle; her yellow body like fine rotten strands of seaweed. Her head had gone.

It was a wonder those great garbage cleaners of the ocean, the sharks, hadn't taken all of her. Like most Australians Sophie feared the grey nurses and white pointers, though she had fancied, as a little girl, spiders. She smiled at the memory of herself at seven trudging to school with a redback spider in a jam jar. Teacher had smiled nervously at the offering for Nature Study and explained, which Sophie already knew, that the redback spider's bite could be fatal to children. Then she had locked it in a cupboard, and each day the teacher and Sophie had gone back to see if it were dead.

Rather like Rosie Dunn, imprisoned in the glass of memory, and each day Ruth and Charlie Dunn, Janet Craig, Rufus Stone and Jim Stokes would take her out to see if she had lost her final powers.

Sophie glanced at her hands. They were quite clean. And the murderers had long ago washed theirs.

Sophie drove home and rang Ruth Dunn. 'So, Ruth,' said Sophie. 'Tell Charlie Janet Craig had some papers. I now have them. I can go for Jim Stokes and that's probably the best solution. By the way, I'm not a lesbian, so please confine yourself to more reasonable statements about your employees.'

There was a long moment's silence.

'I'll get Charlie.' Ruth put down the phone with a jarring crash.

Charlie came to the phone, unperturbed by whatever Ruth was emoting. 'So the point, Charlie,' said Sophie, doing a quick run down, 'is this. If the information contains indictable offences, I'm obliged to go to the Attorney General. Then, of course, it all goes public.'

Charlie Dunn thought for a moment. Then he replied, 'But I won't be going public, and you can wait until you see a bit more. I mean, whoever Jim Stokes is, he can be held on ice, can't he?'

Sophie half-smiled to herself. She was also tempted to burst the bubble on Rosie Dunn, but there was no point. Charlie didn't want to know how Rosie was, only how she had died. 'I can do it, Charlie. Until I can't.'

'That's the way,' replied Charlie. 'Good girl.' He coughed. When he had finished Sophie completed the summary of the day's events. 'Good! Good!' There was a moment's silence. 'Well,' said Charlie heartily, 'Ruth's got supper on the table. Looks like a breast of chicken. Ruth's been doing an Italian cooking course. Turns out pretty well, too, the Italian stuff.'

'OK Charlie, I'll meet Ruth when I've read the papers.'

'Great,' said Charlie. 'Now I'll love you and leave you.'

'Thanks, Charlie.' Sophie hung up, wincing.

Ruth Dunn looked at Sophie across the half-metre of tea shop table at the New Edition bookshop. It was up on Oxford Street and like one of those happy marriages of interests that Sophie remembered from around the Boul' Miche. In between dodging gas grenades and throwing a few cobblestones herself she'd sat in a place like this in 68 with a young revolutionary. He still sent a card now and then to his Chère Sophie. Today he was a Socialist deputy, married with two kids and disapproving of *le canard enchaîné*.

Outside were the glitter kids in their bright pastels. Inside the shops, the tubular steel and white walls dimmed with the greying sky.

'So what is it, this information, Sophie?' Ruth sipped on her cup of tea. Sophie surreptitiously added some brandy from her silver hip flask to her black coffee. Ruth pinched her lips but couldn't fault Sophie's coiffure nor her suit, a smart little number in tweed.

'First cold day this autumn,' opined Sophie. Ruth, wearing another twinset and pearls, nodded.

The tables were close together but mainly unoccupied at eleven on a Thursday morning. It had taken Sophie, between research and phone calls, until now to put together the dossier and to check the facts. The papers were all duplicated and placed in a locker at Central Station. Tomorrow she would fly to Canberra, but that was something she didn't intend to tell Ruth Dunn.

'So what have you to tell me?' asked Ruth Dunn again, disconcerted by her silence.

Sophie decided to put her own questions first.

'Why haven't you and Charlie re-rented Rosie's apartment? It's money, after all.'

Ruth Dunn looked surprised. 'Until the coroner's verdict we felt there was no point in rushing anything. It will come on the market in a month or two.'

'You know, Ruth, Janet Craig kept the papers Rosie gave her. But Janet never mentioned what she knew at the inquest.'

Sophie didn't mention the theatrical retrieval of the papers from the chimney, where they had obviously been placed sometime earlier in the day.

'She also thinks Rosie might have hidden more stuff in her flat.'

Ruth Dunn jumped, but her reply was surprising. 'Well, you can look. That's part of your job. But please don't break in. Come to me for the key.'

Sophie nodded and opened the file. 'It's full of anomalies. Papers and photos of Rufus Stone, Rosie Dunn and a man called Jim Stokes.'

Sophie gave Ruth a brief account of Jim Stokes. Ruth compressed her lips. Somewhere inside, again, she was frightened.

'It all points to Jim Stokes being a front man for Rufus Stone. Meetings, contacts and five small lists. It's all spelled out, Ruth. Rosie was nobody's fool.'

'I know,' said Ruth, again unexpectedly.

Sophie filed away the remark.

'The lists, probably *short* lists, are interesting, since they fit in with the thesis that Janet Craig expounded. Of a shake-up in the underworld. The deaths were Chinese, Thai, two Anglos and one Lebanese. Apparently they'd resisted a consolidation. Rosie wrote down the dates of the meetings, the names of the hit men and the amount paid.

'Behind all of that was Jim Stokes. He in turn must have

been the front man for Rufus Stone. But Stone, Ruth, is never mentioned at all. I find that very strange, as a lawyer. That when you've decided to put the knife in – when you decide to rip the bowels out of the ruling emperor – you don't name him, try at least to include some documentary evidence.

'Rosie must have had it, Ruth, because she slept with him and was dangerous enough to be killed. Or was it just that Rosie was developing a case point by point, like a good essay. You know, the introduction, the body of evidence, and then the conclusion. But Rufus Stone isn't there in the conclusion. Or is the conclusion in her flat?

'What would you think? What would you think when someone has supposedly given evidence to the Drug Squad but there is no evidence of it arriving. I've checked that, too, through a contact. He has top level entry into the computer. Not there. Not filed. What do you think might be the answer?'

'I'm afraid,' replied Ruth, taking a large sip of tea, 'that I'm not trained in these things.'

'But you have common sense, Ruth!'

'Oh yes,' said Ruth Dunn dryly, 'that I have in large measure, as Charlie says.'

'Then what would you make of it?'

Ruth picked up her bag. 'I don't know. All I know is that Rosie is dead and this investigation should never have taken place.'

'How is Charlie reacting?'

Ruth took out her compact, snapped it open and checked out her face. She applied some powder and snapped it shut again.

'Charlie is excited. One part of him, I think, the little boy part, feels he's back in the *Boys' Own*. Another part is curious about you and what you'll find out and whether you'll survive it. Another part wants vengeance for his daughter. The old pound of flesh.' Ruth looked at Sophie. 'If I thought it would help I would get down on my knees, whatever you wanted, for this not to happen.' She stopped. 'I know how you feel about your brother, but what if Rufus Stone wasn't the one who did it?'

46

Sophie felt herself shaking. 'What do you mean?'

Ruth stood up, her voice rising. 'It's really like a play, isn't it? It's like a bloody farce that will be played through to act three, no matter what. And, no one knows yet who'll be left. You know, like in Shakespeare, alive. Or wounded. Or dead. But then the dead don't care, do they?'

'Sit down, Ruth. You're getting hysterical.'

Ruth pushed in her chair. 'There is no evidence about your brother. I said that to . . . to help you see that you wouldn't care about Rosie if it hadn't been for Rufus Stone. I can understand that. Particularly when your father did what he did. Charlie told me about that. Said it would help us to find out about Rosie. Dear God,' she was close to tears, 'it is such a dirty world. It's as if I'm only now growing up and knowing what other people can do. Sometimes I wish I could just pack my bags and walk out. Find a little house somewhere and adopt a cat.'

'It will all work out, Ruth.'

'No, it won't. You see, you just don't know what you're playing with.'

'What, Ruth?'

Ruth was silent again.

'I'll ring you again in a few days.'

'Please don't, Sophie. Please don't ring. Just do what you have to do and give Charlie what you find out.'

'Charlie is paying, Ruth. If you don't want a progress report, I'll tell him and he can make alternative arrangements.'

Ruth stood for a moment gasping for breath, then found again her centre and slowed down. 'I'm sorry, I don't know what came over me. I suppose losing a child does strange things to you. You never expect it and you never expect it could happen in this way.' She started to walk away, then turned back. 'Have you ever loved anyone?' she asked.

Sophie nodded.

'Then you're lucky,' said Ruth. 'And you've got more intelligence than I ever had. You think you marry sensibly and you stay respectable and have children, but at the end of the day they're just part of your compromise.' She dampened her lips. 'I hope you have happiness. I just wish when I'd been younger I'd known what was important.'

She walked out the door and into the bookshop. Sophie saw her pausing, running her eye along the new titles. She selected the Mountbatten biography, paid and left.

Sophie sat for another two minutes sorting out her impressions. Ruth Dunn was ringing alarm bells hard and fast. She certainly knew more than she would admit. And it concerned Rufus Stone. Ruth was nobody's fool. But there was no way Ruth could be pressured to say what she knew if her family was at stake. It was all she had.

Sophie picked up her bag. Who did Ruth think was driving the car that killed David? She glanced out to the street. Ruth Dunn was getting into her car across the road. She glanced back at Sophie but didn't wave.

◆ 8 ◆

The plane lifted off at ten the next morning, taking Sophie to an appointment that had taken all her skill, push and contacts to arrange. Not to mention going deep into debt for future favours. But it was worth it.

Jim Stokes was the crucial link in whatever had happened to Rosie Dunn – the first solid lead to Rosie's murderers.

Beside her on the floor was her leather attaché case, a gift from Cliffie for last year's birthday. She'd scraped off her name in gold letters that Cliff had had incised as the *piece de résistance*. Claimed they'd come out with the rain and it was all you could do, Cliff. Cliff had sulked but come round. It was time to ring Cliff and play the little woman sad without her protector. Only thing was, Cliff would never believe her. Perhaps claims of the tap washer needing changing in the kitchen? Cliff knew she had weak wrists. That might do the trick.

Sophie drank a cup of airline coffee and lit up a cigarette. She was curious to know who her old mate had dug up. Being a paid up card-carrying member of the Labor Party had its uses. As did old contacts.

Senator Lyndal Barry was now on a Senate committee concerned with national security and had sat in on various other commissions. She was a low-ranking minister, not in the inner cabinet but pushing fast up the ladder towards being Australia's first female Prime Minister, sometime before the year 2000. A tough forty-two-year-old with a pleasant smile and retaining a few old dreams for the arts, not to mention social justice. Within limits, of course, she'd said to Soph. So had ended the first conversation in a couple of years. But she'd done her work and the appointment was set up.

Sophie closed her eyes. Next Tuesday was Rosie Dunn's memorial service, followed by the scattering of her ashes. That was to take place down the harbour, around Camp Cove. That was another time to put on pressure. Jamey, with a video recorder. Just to check up on who came with whom. Like Janet Craig. Who would Janet Craig come with?

Jamey boy had done a good job for her. Solid through Saturday outside the house in Victoria Street from nine until two in the morning. Fifty dollars a day. Fortunately, all made easier by the light outside the front door. Bright enough with the camera she'd lent him. The usual collection of shift-workers and frustrated fantasisers had traipsed up the steps. Most of them pausing under the post while they waited for Lil of the Lamplight to come and let them in. She couldn't see Marlene Dietrich making it big in Victoria Street.

Sophie took the photos from her coat pocket. Eight o'clock, getting a pot and bustling up with a self-satisfied smirk . . . Ladies and gentlemen, I give you Norm from Adelaide! Ten was the next on the assembly line of middle-aged lust. They all were middle-aged. Apart from an elderly gent at one, with white hair, wearing an expensive suit and carrying a briefcase. A nice lawyer she'd met a couple of times at dinner at her parents before they'd been paid off by Rufus Stone. Nice practice, nice kids. Might be useful.

Jamey had his comments, too. Funny, most of them, as Jamey boy had a good street humour.

Sophie began rehearsing her brief, mentally going through, point by point, when she would bring out the photos, when to refer to interviews. All taped, even Ruth Dunn. Dirty but necessary, and lacunae – the pauses, the shifts in conversation speed, the evasions – all told their story. It allowed her, too, in the privacy of her study, to listen and pick up, go into negative capability as Keats had called it:

drift into their minds and see if she made a new connection. Something was surfacing on Ruth Dunn but wouldn't yet come into focus.

Underneath was the dull Australian landscape and ahead, so the pilot informed them, was Canberra.

The rest of the business people gathered up their bits and pieces and fastened their safety belts. Sophie closed her eyes and felt the sweat beading around her middle spine. Nothing to do about it, although the shrink had claimed all sorts of sexual insecurities. That was Freud for you.   •

Sophie mentally guided the plane down and as they landed tried out a couple of brief prayers to her private deity.

She glanced around. No one had noticed.

She picked up the hired car at the airport and drove to what approximated, in a non-city, to downtown.

The appointment was in one of those clinical buildings that you could lift up and plant down in New Delhi or Oklahoma. It was on the third floor and she didn't need any clearance.

The lift went up, the lift doors opened, she stepped on to the carpet and turned left along to Industrial Enterprises. Looked legit. enough as did the secretary, a mature twenty-eight or so, with her bright 'How are you and isn't it a nice day' approach.

She gave her name and followed the secretary along to an office with a solid door. It was opened and she went in. The man sitting in an easy chair was around forty, had thick hands, a muscular chest that put Cliffie to shame and a solid Yorkshire face that might have been marginally bovine except for the eyes. Shrewd and competent. Not ASIO, thought Sophie with relief. Australia's internal security boys were noted for their low IQs and their boy scout paranoia about anything to the left of Genghis Khan.

'I'm Sean Long,' said the representative, 'and I understand you've got some information for me.'

So that had been the Senator's line.

'Not entirely,' Sophie sat down. 'You might say, there could be an exchange of information.' There wasn't any point in asking for his credentials, and Sean Long could sit her out

51

any day of the week. 'In return for certain matters relating to a private investigation that might interest you, I want information on Jim Stokes, his clearance and so on. I want to know what he's doing in Sydney, if he's been under investigation. Things like that.'

'A large order,' commented Sean Long in a slow voice. 'Perhaps you should begin.'

Sophie outlined the case. She filled in on Rosie Dunn and the request. Point by point she went over the case she had developed. She left out some names and she condensed information. She also left nicely judged gaps in information and conclusions.

Sean Long picked up her intention and for the first time a smile played briefly across his lips. 'You're a shrewd bargainer, Miss Parnell. You'd have made a good trial lawyer.'

Sophie sat back while he poured the coffee. She accepted the cup and sugared it.

'You've said quite a lot,' Sean Long continued. 'And our common friend says we can trust you.' He picked up his own cup.

Sophie handed over some of the photographs delivered by Janet Craig. 'That's Jim Stokes with the subject whose death I'm investigating. The other is one of my informants on the case.' Rosie Dunn, looking glamorous, was smiling at the camera. Jim Stokes, red of face and mildly pissed, had his arm around a bar girl. Janet Craig was looking away at something else.

'Ah yes,' said Sean Long, 'Rosie Dunn and Janet Craig.'

Sophie took the point. 'What I want to know is this. Jim Stokes is linked with a visa racket in Thailand, according to my information. Three to five thousand dollars for a bar girl with a nest egg to come down here and make even more money.'

'That's so. It took him three years to develop the contacts. It wasn't known by the Embassy, but for his protection the Ambassador was briefed. You know, in case Jim screwed up along the line.'

'So you know?'

'Yes. It's part of a cover. It's still a cover. Jim took the money – kept what he needed for expenses. The rest went into an account for bribes where they were needed, but now he's back in Sydney, the account's reverted to us.'

'May I ask what the point is?'

'I think you know, Miss Parnell.'

'Heroin traffic to Australia?'

'More, Miss Parnell.' Sean Long handed back the photograph of Rosie Dunn, Janet Craig and Jim Stokes. He paused for a moment at the photograph of Rufus Stone on the raft with Rosie Dunn. 'It's much more, and what you know could help us greatly.'

'I want Rufus Stone.'

Sean Long nodded. 'We also have some information on Rosie Dunn, and her death was noted. Also on Janet Craig.' He looked out the window. 'It's a strange city this one. Bureaucrats, politicians and spies.' He turned back to her. 'What's your axe to grind over Rufus Stone?'

'Personal, Mr Long. But I might say more to Jim Stokes.'

'We expected you might.' Sean Long handed her an envelope. 'He's prepared to see you Saturday. The location and time is printed on the card inside. Of course, I'll deny having ever seen you, as would Jim if anything goes wrong – for you, I mean.'

Sophie handed over a list of addresses and telephone numbers taken from Rosie's pocket diary and more pages of the file Janet Craig had handed over. Sean Long took them and began reading.

'The telephone numbers came from Janet Craig and Rosie's diary. She claimed they were collected by Rosie. As part of the information she left with the Drug Squad. There is no record of it being received.'

Sean Long nodded and left for, Sophie supposed, a photocopying machine.

The telephone list had been easy enough to get. She'd rung an old mate, Norma, now working for Telecom as a senior supervisor. But it had been tough turkey for a bit, though Norma was nicely basted after an offer of a swish dinner at Kinselas and plenty of gossip on Cliffie, the bust-up and what sods men were in general.

Then came Norma's turn. Sophie had clucked along like a Mother Confessor of the feminist movement, garnishing Norma with more on the bad fight she'd had. And how she'd gone through Cliff's diary after he'd started coming home suspiciously late. And now Cliff wanted reconciliation, but it wasn't going to be made easy. She wanted the goods on him first. Sophie put in the knife. Would Norma run the numbers through the computer for names and addresses?

'Yeah, why not?' Norma left the phone for a moment to pour herself another whisky. She returned. 'I mean, Soph, what difference does it make? Half the bloody lines in town are bugged anyway. If it's not ASIO it's the Mafia or the cops or whoever's paying off who at that point in time. Doesn't make much difference, does it?'

Norma decided on co-operation and let out a lady-like burp, a hangover from her Methodist upbringing and her Singapore sex change operation. 'That'll fix the bugger. So when's the dinner and drinky poo, Soph?'

Tactfully, Sophie had suggested on delivery.

Norma had rolled up to Sophie's house looking more female than most, and together they'd gawped over the list. Names that didn't make sense. Three oriental and, as Norma cannily pointed out, could be either sex. Norma had already pondered over one – Sophia Mavrakis. 'I've heard about *her*,' said Norma, lowering her voice. 'She's a bloody witch. All the ethnics go to her. You know, the Greeks and Lebanese and Italians. I *do wonder*, Sophie, what Cliff was going to her for. I mean, she specialises in love potions and hexes. Which do you think, Soph? Maybe he was trying to *arouse* greater interest and when he failed reverted to type. You know, fights, threats, violence. I can remember being like that myself, well in my *early* days before I knew who I *really* was.'

Sophie came back from her thoughts. Sean Long had sent someone in with more coffee.

It had all been true to form, the dinner. Norma dressed in her slinkiest outfit – bright crimson and blue silk, long dangling plastic earrings and a modified punk hairdo. Sophie had worn a foil of severe black with pearls to keep Norma on side.

They'd eaten well and Norma tactfully hadn't noticed Sophie picking up the tab.

Afterwards, they'd sat at the bar and while Sophie was in the ladies, Norma had made her hit. Even better than usual, a French hit. Over from New Caledonia and looking for new investments. All said in the right accent with dark brown eyes, bronzed skin and an expensive silk suit cut in safari style. Sophie had drunk down her marguerita and pleaded an early morning start, and said goodbye to Henri with just a twinge of lust in her belly.

Sean Long returned with her papers. He handed them back and lit up a cigarette. Sean Long, Sophie felt, was beginning to trust her.

'Thanks,' he said. 'It adds another piece to the jigsaw puzzle. It also raises a question for your case, I would think?'

Sophie nodded. 'Why, then, was she killed?'

'Someone . . . some group,' Sean Long chose his words carefully, 'knows that Jim Stokes has information and who he is. This is what your story tells us, and we didn't know that. They would use the information against him if they could, but only if that protected their identity. Perhaps they hoped with Rosie Dunn's death and the information fed to her that her family would act. But . . . there may be another possibility.' Sean Long looked out at the blue sky. 'But that's one you yourself might hit upon.'

'What?'

Sean Long shook his head. 'Privileged information. Very privileged, Miss Parnell. It concerns Rosie Dunn. That's all I can tell you.'

Sophie knew she would get no further. At least, not with Sean Long.

He saw her to the door but didn't come out into the passage. Neither did he bother cautioning her or playing the heavy with the official secrets act.

Sophie sat down briefly in her study when she got home, and by force of habit stared at the line of books – Donne, Marlowe and Shakespeare were at eye level, along with Baudelaire and a host of old leather-covered commentaries picked up around the corner from the British Museum.

The angle-poise lamp was pointed low and the curtains were drawn.

What was Rosie Dunn's connection with Sophia Mavrakis, in the newspapers off and on for her wild predictions, scandals and supposed threats against her life.

Sophie also pondered the cheque that had purchased for Rosie Dunn a large emerald ring. No mention of it in her effects, no mention from Charlie or Ruth. She'd asked the same of Janet Craig. Where had it gone? She allowed her mind to slide and saw a hand. On it a large emerald ring. Whose hand, though? It wouldn't come to her.

She picked up the photo of brother David. Bloody, boring, ordinary David. Red hair, nice eyes, a big jaw. Hadn't made kids, never mowed his own lawn, never come home late to see his wife looking daggers at him, with him pissed. It would have been that kind of life, but he was entitled to his bloody ordinariness.

She reached down for her large bag and took out the Biretta. It was the only case to date where she thought it would be used before the end. She had no idea what its title was.

Guns, it seemed, all had names like cars and their killing capacity calibrated somewhere on the metal. Not really phallic, as they said. Just workman-like. The Biretta had been the suggestion of a mate of David's. From the old days, before David had left the Marists and moved on to better things and been enrolled at Branston. Now the mate was sergeant-in-charge of the police firing range. Sophie had enjoyed the training and found that her wrist was OK. Not many bull's-eyes but close enough to place a shot. Maybe it was time for a refresher course.

The telephone had been hooked in to the machine for a couple of days. She switched on the listen. A couple of unimportant calls. The third was Cliffie with a crackle and pop. 'Hi, Soph, how are ya?' said Cliffie, then had a long think. 'Mum sends her love. She's not as good a cook as you are, Soph.' Long pause. 'Look Sophie, I'm sorry. I don't think you're an old cow.' (Sophie waited for literal Cliff to run through the insults he had employed. It came from those lists kids made when first attending confession.) 'And I don't think you're bloated with booze, you're just large, a real model for one of those painters like Van Gogh.' (Cliff used to read her art books on wet Sunday afternoons. Had he got mixed up with Reubens?)

'I reckon I made a mistake,' went on Clifford Cray. 'It's not the same at home and Mum reckons I'd be better off with you than anyone else.' (No doubt, thought Sophie.) 'I'm kinda missing you, Soph and I promise I'll be a good boy. No more fights, eh, Soph and I've gotta job. Security Guard, starting tomorrow,' (another large bone of contention had been Cliffie's finances) 'and the pay's OK. So I'll be able to give you my keep and a bit over for gas and electricity.' (Wooing had never been Clifford Cray's strong point.) Then Sophie found herself melting. 'And I've written a poem for ya, Soph. Sort of modern. I'm working on another one too, about you. I thought I might pop over tomorrow and read them to you, to get your views. OK then, Soph? See ya tomorrow.' Cliff made kissing noises and hung up.

Sophie did up her old chenille dressing gown and forgot

about Rosie Dunn and Jim Stokes. Humming to herself, she padded along to the kitchen.

And it all happened before she had time to think. All she heard was a soft swish, and the world exploded. At the time she was looking at the gas ring and wondering about the kettle. She felt herself go down, still thinking about the kettle, as if the thought had been driven into her brain centre.

She came to and found her eyes reluctant to open, and when they did she felt drifty, dreamy, peaceful. Like after a good joint. Then she remembered, and the darkness flooded in to give her time to think. Slowly she moved her legs. Not tied. The floor felt like her own linoleum and the light, a dying sun somewhere in the kitchen cosmos, was her own light. She waited again for a voice, or a gun against her temple or back. Nothing happened.

She pulled herself on to her hands and knees and began crawling up the hall. She counted to herself to relieve the fear that somewhere someone was watching and waiting. Playing her like a cat with its mouse. Ready to move at the right moment when she thought herself safe.

She got to the study and found her bag on the floor. The contents were scattered about, but the Biretta was still within clutching distance. She reached for it, checked the chambers, clicked off the safety and dialed Cliff's number.

Cliff growled and slammed the phone down. Out of the house, Sophie guessed muzzily, before she'd have time to remember even what day of the week it was. She stayed where she was.

Sometime later, a week, a few hours later, (Cliff said twenty minutes), the key went into the door. To be sure, Sophie raised the Biretta and rested it against the upturned chair.

Cliff ran in, stopped and looked down the barrel. Sophie sighed.

'Take it, Cliff. Check the house, top to bottom.'

Cliff went through the rooms while she floated off. Sometime later she felt Cliff's long hands about her. 'I'll get you an aspirin and whisky, Soph.' Sophie sat. Cliff started on an old diatribe about security in Paddo, the junkies down at the Cross, then changed his mind. He went and made up an icepack. By the sound of it, he was using a hammer. Applied to the nape of her neck, the ice steadied Sophie.

'Do you want a doctor, Soph?'

Sophie looked around for her address book. The telephone black book was on her desk. 'Ring Golda, my Jewish mate. She'll hold her tongue.'

Cliffie rang. Golda squawked and was in the house a quarter of an hour later, long black wet hair wrapped in a towel. She did a thorough check. 'Looks OK. Could do with an X-ray but I don't think there's any trauma.' She shone her pinpoint torch into Sophie's eyes. Checked again. Waited, took blood pressure and picked up her bag.

'I'll send you a cheque,' said Sophie.

'Forget it,' said Golda, mouth tight. 'Just hope you get the bastard.'

'You up to it, Soph?' asked Cliff. 'The stairs, I mean?' Sophie nodded. They walked along the hall, Cliff tugging her towards the bottom step like a sheepdog running a sheep. That alerted Sophie. She stopped.

'The front room, Cliff?'

'Shit!' Cliff resigned himself and followed Sophie, supporting her as best he could. Sophie walked in and sat down again. But wasn't going to oblige the gods by weeping.

The Brett Whiteley had been slashed right across the Harbour Bridge, and slashed again diagonally, then hacked at in short bursts of spite. The chairs had been covered in red wine and the books pulled out and similarly treated. The bottles lay on the floor. Only the Norman Lindsay remained unscathed.

'Let's go to bed, Cliff.'

Helped up the stairs, Sophie arrived in the bedroom.

'You've turned into a real lazy cow,' said Cliff feigning good cheer. 'A real slack tart. Look at the bed. When did you last make it?'

Sophie knew what had happened, but Cliff had a strange turn of working-class Catholic prudery so she didn't enlighten him yet. While she had been unconscious on the kitchen floor, someone, two people, had been screwing after their small

59

debauch in the rest of the house. Maybe even while she rang Cliff they were leaving. They must have let themselves out the front door.

'How did they get in, Cliff?'

'Back door. Cut the glass and opened it.'

Cliff stripped the sheets, made up the bed, helped Sophie out of her dressing gown and piled up the pillows. 'Sorry,' said Cliff, 'that we get back together like this.'

'Doesn't matter, mate,' replied Sophie, much comforted.

Cliff locked the bedroom door. He stripped down only as far as his underpants in token of the formality of the night and got into bed and held Sophie's hand and made soothing noises. Sophie put the Biretta on to the night table and drifted off again. Cliff, on his back, hand tight in Soph's and trying to sleep light, started a nervous snore.

The phone rang at three. Sophie switched on the recorder and picked it up. Cliff sat bolt upright, a puzzled look on his face.

'OK,' said a woman's voice with an overlay of what might be American, 'you've had your warning. Next time you play for keeps. Keep your nose out of things. Rosie Dunn's dead and gone and in her grave.'

'Oh yeah, mate.' Sophie felt a fine, wonderful anger bubbling up. 'Just listen to me. You trash my house and I'll trash you, one way or another.'

'Keep your nose out or you'll regret it.' The voice had changed quality. It was cold, deadly and certain. 'Don't interfere. Just cut your losses.'

Suddenly it clicked into place. Sean Long, Ruth Dunn and Janet Craig. It all fitted, and Sophie only just restrained herself. 'Who are you?' she asked, now knowing the answer.

There was a long pause at the other end and the woman laughed.

Then the line went dead.

Sophie lay back, the adrenalin coursing, the headache masked by it.

'I've got a call to make now, Cliff.' Sophie had memorised the number. It rang quite a few times. Ruth Dunn answered.

'Put me on to Charles,' said Sophie, not wasting words. Charlie came on.

'Charlie, have you a recording of Rosie. You know, the sort of thing kids do. A message, a tape from Thailand?'

'Yes,' said Charlie. 'There's one in her room.'

'Good, Charlie. I want you to bring it around now.'

'Now?'

'Yes, Charlie, and ask Ruth to bring it in. I want to have a sort of woman's talk.'

'At bloody three o'clock in the morning.'

'Yes, Charlie. Something's happened. Something very important. And, Charlie, this isn't the *Boy's Own Annual*, you know. Nor am I going to die for the cause, Charlie.'

There was silence. 'What do you mean?' asked Charlie Dunn.

'Life is real, life is in earnest, Cousin Charles.' Sophie hung up and let Cliff in on the developments.

Cliff sat there, face pale and drawn, puffing nervously on their communal fag until it was at the filter. 'Jesus,' said Cliff as she finished. 'It's like something out of the movies.'

'But evidence, Cliff. Evidence. I've got to remember I'm doing this as a case. Not as a policeman. But, I'm being played, Cliff, and I don't like it.'

'I can see that, Sophie.'

'What could the motive be, Cliff? There's always a motive.'

The bell rang.

'Put on your smart dressing gown Cliff, and let the lady in. I'm going to have to receive in bed. My head won't take the stairs.'

Cliff got into Sophie's chenille effort, and loped off. 'Show her first my front room, Cliff,' Sophie called out.

Three minutes by the bedside clock Ruth Dunn appeared wearing an old duffle coat over a pair of slacks. Both must have dated back to her own student days, thought Sophie.

Cliff was at the door. Sophie nodded. He shut the door leaving the women alone.

'Give it to me, Ruth.'

Ruth handed over the cassette.

Sophie put it down on the duvet.

'Tonight I was knocked out, all the papers on Rosie Dunn taken. While I was coming around the thieves were having it off in my bed. Then, a while ago, there was a phone call.'

Ruth licked her lips. 'What did they say?'

'Nothing much, Ruth. But the woman who made it was high, really high. On adrenalin. That walking the thin line, that waving of the red cape while you wait for the bull to charge. She must be quite a matador, mustn't she, Ruth?'

Ruth sat down heavily.

'Charlie came home and vomited, all that night after seeing her. Then he wept and vomited most of the next day. I thought he was going to go over the edge. But he didn't. He recovered.'

'Isn't Rosie Dunn dead, Ruth?'

Ruth sat tight lipped. She looked at the cassette in Sophie's hand. 'You know, when Charlie told me what he'd decided, I begged. I got down on my knees.' Ruth glanced at Sophie's flannel nightie. 'That was the night he employed you.

'He hit me, not once, a lot of times. He was drunk, of course. But he thought he had a reason. A memory. He called me a cold-hearted bitch. A manipulator, a ball breaker, a cunt. He called me a lot of names and he beat me. You know,' she looked at Sophie, 'as they do in movies – to women – or, as they say, out in the working-class suburbs. He said he had to know why his Rose had died.' Ruth looked bleakly at Sophie. 'You don't understand. You must stop.'

Sophie pulled herself up on the pillows. 'I don't like being played with.'

Ruth Dunn shook her head gently. 'Charlie wouldn't want it.'

'I want it!' Sophie lit up a cigarette. 'You are right. I'll probably never nail Rufus Stone. But I'll find out whatever happened to Rosie Dunn. The reason, Ruth. The motive.'

'Never.' Ruth Dunn gathered up herself and smiled at the tape. 'You'll never find out what happened.'

'So you are now a belligerent, Ruth?'

Ruth Dunn walked to the door. 'I'll tell Charlie you were

broken in on tonight. I'll explain you were deeply upset. I'll say that you were suffering concussion.'

She opened the door.

Sophie saw Cliff on the stairs.

Then the door closed and Cliff escorted Ruth Dunn to the front door.

Sophie felt the headache returning.

10

It was ten the following morning. Sophie sat in her study. The headache was less. Cliffie had made coffee and toast and sat with her in his security guard uniform, all navy-blue and buckled. Sophie put in the tape Ruth had given her and winced. Loud music issued forth.

'Who is it, Cliff?' she asked.

'Boy George,' guessed Cliff.

Sophie turned it down. They sat through twenty minutes.

'Same,' said Cliff with a giggle. 'Bloody little twat.'

'OK Cliff, I know you're a poet in the making.' Which was true, she thought. The poems weren't half bad.

Sophie sipped on her coffee. 'Why, Cliff?'

Cliff was used to these interrogations of the soul. Sophie was the same every time as things started to draw to a conclusion.

'I dunno,' Cliff looked at the cassette as it wound over another pain-provoking track.

'I'll tell you. No, I won't tell because I don't know. I'll tell you what I do know. The tape is gone forever and Ruth Dunn, as she says Charlie has said of her, has a lot of common sense. She knows I can't go to Charlie since I've got no proof. Charlie Dunn believes in what's been set in front of him. If I said Ruth had destroyed the tape . . . that she acted at once, since she worked it out, he'd laugh. Ruth Dunn is a dull woman, an ordinary mother. Nothing special. If I said

Rosie Dunn is alive he'd ask me to produce her. If I said well, where is the tape?, he'd say I don't know. Maybe it got thrown out or lost. Ruth made a mistake.

'If I say Ruth Dunn's a liar he'd throw a fit. Ruth Dunn is his wife and an honorary prop in the scrum. He'd say what proof have you got?'

'Well, what proof have you got?' asked Cliff.

'None. I'm working on intuition. Something about Janet Craig and her feeling for Rosie. It wasn't the feeling you have for someone dead. It was a feeling for someone alive. I know Cliff, since I loved David and he's dead. Then, Ruth. Frightened by a ghost, as she called Rosie. No, not a ghost. But why Cliff? Why did Rosie Dunn die and why did she *need* to die?'

'Why did you wait until now?' asked Cliff. 'Just call around and ask Charlie Dunn for the tape. You'd have it now. All the proof.'

Sophie listened to the last song. It was about a love affair and searching and depression and pills. It was apposite.

'No, no voice expert can confirm *that* absolutely. For one you get in court on your side, Cliff, you'll have another to cast doubts and say, this and that phoneme and that vowel point to someone else. And, Cliff it's not a court. It's a paid-for investigation. How would I prove it with that American accent. How would I prove to Charlie Dunn that the bloated carcass he looked at was not his daughter but a stand-in. That Rosie Dunn whom he loves never loved him? He wouldn't believe it. I needed something concrete Cliff, and I got it. Ruth changed the tapes and confirmed it all.'

Sophie picked up the phone and rang Ruth Dunn. 'I've thought about it, Ruth. You're probably right. I think what I'll do is this. Play it along for a week or two, and then tell Charlie that I can't go on.'

'I have some money,' said Ruth. 'If he asks for his fee back, simply agree. I'll make sure it's made up.'

'OK Ruth.' Sophie sounded, even to herself, defeated, sad and tired.

'It's for the best,' said Ruth. 'It's best to leave these things alone.'

'OK Ruth,' Sophie sighed. 'There's no point is there, in ending up on a slab myself.'

'No.' Ruth's voice was quietly pleased.

'So, I'll hand in the report to Charlie in a couple of weeks. In the meantime I'll make a few waves and leave it there.'

'I'm sorry about the house.' Ruth paused. 'When we're both old I'll tell you about it.'

'I understand, Ruth,' Sophie went into her best method training, 'and I've decided to leave it.'

Ruth paused. 'I'm pleased – for all of us.'

Sophie said goodbye, wearily, and replaced the receiver.

'Jesus.' Cliff looked wide-eyed as an owl. 'You slack tart.'

'Exactly, Cliff. It gives me breathing space. I'm going to need it.'

11

Sophie mulled over the case while she drove on automatic pilot along the Bondi freeway. Ruth Dunn was the linch-pin, the pivot, the sad and ailing whore, selling herself for family honour. And the question to ask Ruth Dunn today was simple. 'Are you going to tell Rosie, Ruth, that I know?'

Ruth, as Sophie brought her into focus in her head, looked this way and that and picked up her cup of tea and sipped decisively. 'No,' she said, 'my daughter is dead.'

'What is she blackmailing you with, Ruth. Just her death? Or, is it something more?'

Ruth sat in Sophie's head in her garden and looked at a kookaburra diving at the goldfish in her pond. Her hands were twisting on her lap and on her face was a look of pure pain. The kind a mother once might have had for a child who grew up to hammer the nails into Christ. 'So,' thought Sophie to herself remembering that look from the bookshop meeting, 'there's more. There has to be more.'

'Is Rosie in Sydney still, Ruth?'

Ruth didn't look at Sophie. Maybe Ruth didn't know.

'But Rosie was in Sydney the night my house was trashed, wasn't she Ruth? It was Rosie who rang up, wasn't it? And it was Rosie and Rufus Stone who had it off in my bed?'

Ruth nodded and looked back at the kookaburras.

'And Ruth, the other card I hold is the addresses. You see that little diary you gave me when we met up at Paddington

Market contained numbers. They were scattered here and there in the middle of trivia. She'd have made a good resistance worker, Ruth. She has, class, Rosie. But she forgot about them.

'Now, as I was saying, among them were numbers – those of three Chinese. Two of them are now dead. I believe they were the ones supplying Rosie for her dealing. The ones Janet Craig mentioned, en passant. And that's what Rufus Stone found out about.

'I suspect Jim Stokes will confirm that the Chinese and Thais were using Rosie to get at Rufus Stone. A little internal war, but Rufus found out. Rosie suffered but was reinstated. And then the contracts were put out and the dissidents put down.'

Sophie felt herself cheering up. There were quite a few cards to play before the game finished. Sophie came off automatic and lit up a Gauloise. They made a change from the Virginia tobacco but Sophie's windbag lungs didn't agree. They coughed.

What would Jim Stokes have to say this afternoon? The meeting was arranged at Bronte Beach, down by the saltwater pool. Sophie had driven over and checked out the location.

She switched back to Rufus Stone and Rosie Dunn. The bed scene – and that was no fantasy – was equally a vital clue to the hidden life of Rufus and Rosie. As was the break-in itself. After all, why expose yourself to danger? Logically that is.

She wondered then what house-cleaning Jim Stokes and his friends, like Sean Long, would be implementing. Quite a bit. They ran a racket outside the authority of any parliamentary act. Smear Jim Stokes and you smashed at one go the evidence against Rufus Stone. Or was it so?

She shivered as if a goose was walking over her grave. Then Rosie Dunn came back into her mind. A much fleshed-out Rosie Dunn. Would Ruth ever tell Rosie that Sophie knew about her? Sophie tried to imagine how Rosie looked now. Different in physical shape – truly what she was in spirit.

No Ruth Dunn wouldn't tell. She was an old-style

conservative who evaded reality as her husband evaded taxes. She wouldn't tell Rosie she was off the slab – since somewhere, deep down, Ruth Dunn hated Rosie Dunn.

Sophie changed lanes for Bondi Beach, ignoring the irate hooting of a Mercedes. Over one hill was the beach. The sand would be white and sparkling and in the sea the surfies waiting those long high Pacific swells. But it wasn't the beach she was coming for but Sophia Mavrakis, the witch.

She hung out in Illawong Avenue, noted for its burned-out thirties architecture in shades of brick. Sophie had been to the road before, to her blind Jewish doctor who cured people of smoking by hypnotism. 'Such a strong resistance, dear,' Hilda had said in her strong post-Buchenwald Oz accent, and given up on the cure.

Sophie parked the car and walked up a concrete path flanked on either side by a lawn. On a burned space stood a barbecue and some dog turds. It didn't look as if Sophia Mavrakis' contact with the beyond had helped her in elementary aesthetics.

Sophie pressed the doorbell and gazed thoughtfully at the acid-etched stag at bay. Symbol, of course, of Apollo. Inside she knew how it would be and she was right. The marks of the spirit were evident in the technicolour palmtrees that framed Sophia Mavrakis as she opened up to the formica bright sitting room, where she was met by several cross-eyed and vexed Byzantine saints emitting powerful light from their mean eyes. On a small table was draped a black cloth, and on the cloth a crystal ball. Beside the ball was an incense burner. Beside the burner a pack of tarot cards. There was a strange smell in the air which reminded Sophie of something. Horses being shod, the red hot shoe held against the hoof. Burnt nail clippings, that was it.

'You've just had a customer, Sophia?' asked Sophie.

Sophia arched an eyebrow and stared intently at the table.

Sophia Mavrakis, so she claimed in her press interviews, was of ancient Greek extraction. One of the blood of the colonies of Magna Graecia that had produced the great temples at Paestum and, at a later date, Sophia Mavrakis of somewhere around Naples. Sophia Mavrakis also claimed to have been born during an earthquake that had destroyed the village but left her and her family alive with the house standing. All was possible. Sophie mentioned their common Christian name.

'Yes,' said the Signora Mavrakis or Kyria Sophia, depending on the client. 'It means wisdom. For me that came at an early age. Now you sit down.' Sophia Mavrakis was obviously used to clients who didn't give their full names.

Sophie sat down on a hard wooden chair.

'Yes, at an early age. My father was in touch with the Black Arts and I was very young. But then the Virgin vouchsafed me a vision of Herself. Then she told me I had great powers for good and would bind many forces.'

Presumably, thought Sophie again looking around, one of the forces hadn't been good taste.

'So what is it you have come to ask?' Sophia, weasel face intent, lit two white candles and then two black candles taken from under the table. 'This,' she announced, not waiting for a reply, 'represents good and evil.' She lit the fifth candle, a delicate pink. 'This represents the Spirit of Guidance who reigns supreme in our sphere of life.'

Sophie reached into her bag for a cigarette, lit it and sat back.

Sophia Mavrakis was surprised. It wasn't your usual reaction to a summoning of the powers.

'Please do not smoke, it affects the spirits.'

Sophie dug around in her bag. Searched for her private investigator's licence. Tried to remember when she'd seen it last. It had been in her bag until the night her house was trashed. She stowed the thought for later reference.

'I'm a private investigator, Sophia.'

Sophia drew back, cold, aloof and pure.

Sophie took out five ten-dollar notes and placed them on the table. 'I've come for a consultation.' The usual fee, she knew, was twenty-five dollars.

'OK, OK dear, what izzit? Someone complaining their boyfriend's died, or someone's still pregnant? Accidents

70

happen you know. Specially when the client doesn't respect the Forces.'

Sophie took out two photos and placed them face down on the tablecloth.

Sophia Mavrakis' eyes kept darting to them and then settled on the money.

'It won't cause any problems, Sophia. It's about a client you saw once.'

'Yeah, well,' Sophia picked up the notes and turned over the photos. They were of Rosie Dunn, Janet Craig and Rufus Stone.

'All of them might have consulted you within the last eighteen months.'

Sophia Mavrakis, descendant of a proud race, squeezed her eyes, pursed her lips and attempted mystery with her eyes. It failed, Sophie decided, lamentably.

'Yeah, well, she probably did. The blonde one, I mean. Pretty kid.'

'What did she want?' Sophie pulled deep on her Gauloise and suppressed a cough. She kept her eyes on the clairvoyant but was outfoxed by a well-tried expert.

Sophia reached into her own pocket and took out a packet of Benson and Hedges, selected one, lit up, sat back and stared at the ceiling.

'Yeah, well, dear, a client's mystery is a client's mystery.'

Sophie added another fifty. 'Did you see her here or down at the Cross?'

'At the Cross, dear. I've gotta lot of connections around there. Hear a lot, you see, and know a lot of people.'

'So what did she want?'

'Yer, well, you've gotta think about things in my business. Like, reincarnation. It's hard to understand attraction between two people, and sometimes a girl will try out something.'

'Rosie Dunn?'

'Yeah, well, yes,' Sophia Mavrakis for a moment looked embarrassed. 'Yeah, well, I guessed, somehow.'

'What?'

'Well, I can't say. If the client should hear!'

71

'Hear? The client is dead, Mrs Mavrakis. Your client, I mean. I don't imagine you've got to worry about her.'

'Dead?' Sophia Mavrakis stroked her dyed blonde hair and started to titter. 'Dead? That wasn't on the cards from what *I* could see.'

'She jumped off the Gap, or maybe was thrown.'

Sophia Mavrakis pulled her chair forward, picked up the tarot cards and started to shuffle. 'A lot of strange things happen. Maybe I was asked for a contact for a job. Nothing too big, but big enough. She paid me good money. Maybe death was around.' Sophia pulled Death out of the pack, studied its skeletal form, and placed it face upwards. 'But then again, in a manner of speaking, maybe it wasn't.'

'It's come already,' said Sophie, playing dumb.

'Sure, sure.' Sophia put down the pack.

'Are you involved in the drug traffic?'

'Drugs?' For the first time Sophia Mavrakis became real. 'Bloody perverts. They all ought to be shot. Killing kids and perverting people. I'd put the bloody lot against a wall. Not that you don't see people. Professionally, that is.'

Sophie Parnell sat back, believing. 'What did you do for Rosie Dunn then?'

Sophia flicked her nail against a ten-dollar note. 'It's past history, but only in a way. One thing she asked for remains private.' She paused. 'Maybe the other might come back into me head, though. She wanted one thing that remains private and when I approached the oracles they said OK. Strange but OK. Must be karmic. So she got me what I needed.'

'What?'

'Oh well, articles of personal clothing, a bit of hair.'

'What sort of hair?'

'Yer, well, when you're working on earth forces you've gotta be where it's at.'

That, thought Sophie Parnell, was probably the object of quite a few consultations. She placed another twenty down. 'And the other request?'

'I've gotta think.' The strain was making Sophia oscillate between several potential personalities floating like fragments in the nebula of her brain. 'It was a difficult bit of work. Not so much for me,' said Sophia to the Byzantine saints. 'But I've gotta think. And if I say "yes", it'll cost.'

'How much?'

'Two thousand,' said Sophia. 'And you keep your mouth shut and where you got the information. But, first, I've gotta think. And, you don't come here no more.'

Sophie gave her her card.

'OK, OK. I'll consult the stars, check things out. I'll work out some place where we can talk if the cards say "Yes".'

Sophie stood up. 'When?'

'Tomorrow,' said Sophia. 'I'll give ya a ring tomorrow. But not here. And, I'll name the rendezvous. Somewhere, yer, maybe, that'll be the place.'

'Where?'

'Wait and see. Nothin's decided yet. But if it is, it'll be down at the Domain. Dame Joan's singin' in *The Tales of Hoffman*. Plenty of people around. And besides,' said Sophia Mavrakis, 'I used to study voice – in the old days!'

❖ ❖ ❖

Sophie pulled the car into the kerb at Bronte Beach and turned off the engine. She didn't bother looking out yet but stared straight ahead.

Sophia Mavrakis had been a rich, if erratic, field to till. What she could answer was not so important. She wouldn't get her two thousand dollars either. Around five hundred, Sophie calculated, would do the trick. The rest was simply the exaggeration of an overtaxed ego boosting its market value.

What she knew was simple. Where the body had come from. What had she said? 'Death was around. But only in a manner of speaking.' A headless corpse was death in a manner of speaking. Identified only by a ring on the hand since the authorities had no dental records. But Sophie still had to know, precisely, the details. How and when and who had been found. How it had been arranged.

She looked sideways. Her eyes were stunned for a moment by the swells, the rocks, the expanse of beauty that lapped this inner city of Sydney and the suburb of Bronte.

Down there was a hollow of green that stretched back into a flowing uphill expanse of grass. Dotted around were huts and barbies where the Greeks, Italians and Lebanese could crouch and enact their latest destiny. Beyond was the sea and a wall where they could walk, and below a stretch of sand, usually packed in summer but now hollowed down by the high tide.

To the side the Bronte Baths where Jim Stokes and she would meet. That was what had been written on the card Sean Long had given her in Canberra. She supposed he was there already, since she was ten minutes late.

She got out of the car and walked stolidly across the road, down the path and approached the Baths. She stood looking. It was all whitewashed: the rocks above the pool, the enclosure, the pool itself. It was clean, simple and very beautiful as the waves pounded in from the rocks beyond and hit against the concrete and plunged along the line into the pool, surging, hitting against the wake of the last and the thrust of the new.

Sophie smiled into the tumult and then saw the coat floating, knocking, winding and retreating and again picked up and thrust this way and that like something in a washing-machine. She stopped at the rail and peered down and saw that the coat held more than water.

She turned quickly, but the esplanade was empty of everything but a couple of dogs and at the far end a jogger, vanishing up the rise that would lead to the cliffs above Tamarama Beach.

The waves again caught the coat and dashed the body against the concrete. Then they left it by itself in a moment of calm, and it turned face up. Sophie peered down at it to check what she already knew.

The face was that of Jim Stokes and there was no point wading in or thinking of mouth-to-mouth resuscitation. The mouth was open and had been for some time. And besides, as it turned again, she saw the dark stain further down on the white shirt. Jim Stokes had been shot, not drowned.

She turned quickly, checking the cliff walk above.

'Jesus!' She pulled herself together. 'You're twittering worse than Norma,' she told herself. She walked slowly back to the road. In the distance rain squalls were approaching and the gates to the pool, which should have been closed on such a day to protect the ignorant or the brash, swung to and fro. She reached the blue beat-up Volkswagon, climbed in, lit a cigarette, took the silver flask from the glove box, opened it and pulled deep on the brandy, switched on the ignition, put her foot on the accelerator and turned fast and up the hill.

Ten minutes later she was in Regent Street and then in her house and dialling the Canberra number of the Export Business. An hour later she caught up with Sean Long. She gave him the information. He listened and took details. Then he hung up. She hung up around one minute later since she could not release her grip on the black Bakelite phone handle.

Obviously Sean Long hadn't had time to organise the salvage operation, since the next morning the death was reported as murder.

That evening, as she watched the television coverage of the Baths, she waited for mention of suspects. None came. No mention of a blue Volkswagon, no mention of anything. But then, right at the end, the question was dropped. Was this a drugs-related murder? The following morning the *Sydney Morning Herald* claimed an unnamed source who had suggested Jim Stokes had been involved in a visa scam in Thailand while working in the consulate, and was known to have drug connections there and in Sydney.

No one came forward to contradict.

❖ ❖ ❖

Sophie got herself dressed. This morning was Rosie Dunn's memorial service. Jamey would be outside the church, camera at the ready. She was to meet Sophia Mavrakis that evening, and it wouldn't hurt to have Jamey along there, too.

Sophie called for a taxi.

Five minutes after stepping into it she stepped out at the Anglican Church in Ocean Street, which was appropriate enough. Sophie hurried up the path, entered, dropped a genuflection and remembered where she was. She slipped into a wooden pew at the back. Up the front the minister was talking to a white-haired woman at the organ.

No candles had been lit, and that must mean the church was not prepared to say Rosie Dunn had gone out in the manner befitting, but was prepared to offer social support.

The front pews filled up, then the family came in. Ruth's face, severe: make-up, a dab of powder and lipstick. Behind her, her two children. The son was dressed in a black suit and must by now be at medical school himself. The girl was crying. Charlie held himself erect as if on hospital rounds.

The minister knelt, and the congregation shuffled about as it decided on the most appropriate position.

The prayers were in modern English and had none of the majesty Sophie remembered from Chamfield. The organ struck up a moment later. It was the 'Twenty-Third Psalm'. Anyone could muddle along to that. Sophie muddled, intimidated by the space, and then froze. Entering a far back pew was Rufus Stone. With him was a woman. Then, the memory clicked into place. The same woman who had been walking down at the Opera House. The woman with the faint American accent.

Sophie froze deeper. Ruth Dunn turned around, and her face froze too.

Sophie moved around the side and out through the open baize door and over to the car. She got into the driving seat and sat for a moment looking at her hands.

'What is it, Soph?' asked Jamey, dressed in jeans and an old cord jacket.

'I want you to follow the two who came in late.'

Jamey nodded.

'Just keep behind them, wherever they go. If they split up, follow the woman.'

'What are you doing?'

'Family.' Sophie looked austere. 'I'll go with the family. For the ceremony on the harbour.'

❖ ❖ ❖

The boat was anchored in Camp Cove, a hundred yards from the shore. Charlie, now not on public view, held his daughter and wept. Ruth, white-faced, looked down at the still mirror of the water. Sophie, at the prow, looked at the shoreline.

The surviving daughter, what was her name? Heather? took out a piece of paper and read a poem. Her brother listened. It was about the victory over death. John Donne. Sophie was surprised. Heather, she supposed, had studied English Literature. Then the brother read a piece he'd written himself about Rosie Dunn. About youth, young life cut off and the beauty of the sea: the sea of eternity, the sea of faith. Unconscious memories of Robert Browning's 'Dover Beach'.

Sophie moved back into the shelter of the cabin. All eyes were now on the box that cousin Charles was picking up. It was of simple unpolished wood. Cousin Charles didn't have any words and the language of the sea sufficed with the high gulls.

Sophie took out her high-powered pocket binoculars, useful on a couple of divorce cases where friendly separation was out of the question. She focused on the cliff above Camp Cove then swept slowly along the beach to the lawn of the last house and stopped.

Cousin Charles nodded to the captain.

The engine was turned on and slowly they moved out and the ashes left the box and scattered in grey on to the water behind them, floating on the wake then vanishing into the swells.

Sophie raised the glasses for one last glance. They were still there at the lawn's edge. The woman had binoculars in her hand and was laughing like a young bride, her arm through Rufus Stone's. On her finger Sophie caught a glint of green. She refocused and the ring came into view. It was indeed a fine emerald.

She went back to the family, in her role as Cousin Sophie representing Cousin Terence and Cousin Thelma, up at their retirement apartment on the Gold Coast. She offered quietly her condolences. Ruth managed a half smile but could not take her eyes off the beach. Charlie dabbed his eyes with a white handkerchief. The children looked at the view and a white handkerchief. The children looked at the view and muttered thanks.

Sophie walked by herself to the prow. Ruth took note as Charlie followed her.

'So,' asked Charlie, belligerent in his grief. 'When do we get results?'

'I'm seeing a woman tonight, Charlie. A woman called Sophia Mavrakis. She had some sort of reputation as a clairvoyant. Rosie saw her over a year ago.'

'What use is a bloody clairvoyant?'

'She has information, Charlie. She wants two thousand but I'll cut her down to five hundred, if it's worth it. We'll be meeting at the Domain. There's an opera on.'

'So you think you'll get something?'

'Yes I do. I think she's got quite vital ancillary information, Charlie.'

'Ruth,' said Charlie, 'doesn't like you. She says we should never have begun this.'

'What do you think Charlie?'

Charlie looked across to the Harbour Bridge, which they were approaching. 'Rufus Stone came to the funeral with one of his fancy women. Left before I had a chance to belt the bastard.'

'Like a red cape to a bull, Charlie?'

Charlie looked down at his signet ring. 'If you had to, how would you arrange a contract on someone like him, Sophie?'

Sophie took a step backwards. 'I wouldn't Charlie. I really wouldn't even think about it. I'll tell you what happened to Rosie Dunn. Soon.'

'You reckon it'll soon be over.'

Sophie smiled at Ruth walking over the coiled ropes towards them. 'Yes. I think so.'

'Was the tape any use?' asked Charlie. 'You know, Rosie's voice?'

Sophie shook her head. 'Ruth picked up the wrong one.'

'Bloody women,' muttered Charlie. 'You can never rely on them when the going's rough.' He leaned over the rail.

'Sorry about the house being done over. And about what happened to you. Something like that can really scramble your brain for a day or two.'

'I checked it out, Charlie. No real concussion.'

The boat moored and Sophie, smiling at the family and friends, left first and hurried down the wharf.

She arrived at Regent Street twenty minutes later and let herself in the front door.

Cliffie had come off the late-night shift and was in her kimono. He'd shaved himself and cut himself. A piece of loo paper, like dried black skin, hung on to his top lip.

'I've been home to mum's and collected me things. I've also collected George and a mate.'

Sophie looked at the back door, now flat out on the courtyard. The lintel was being lined with steel.

'Jesus, Cliffie, I can't afford this.'

'I've called in a favour.' Cliff looked tense. 'It's a cut-price job. I've also got a recording for when you're out. You turn it on. Anyone coming to the back or front door sets it off.' Cliff turned to a small box, pressed the red button, and put his hand close to it. A crescendo of mad barking echoed around the kitchen. Molly Meldrum, the ginger cat, jumped from his chair, hackles high and eyes popping. 'Tune up old Molly, too,' said Cliff complacently.

Sophie made her phone call while Cliff poured the tea and buttered a scone.

'What's all that about?' Cliff handed Sophie her cup.

'Need a surveillance job on a house, Cliff. Down at Camp Cove.'

'That where she's hanging out, is it?'

'I don't know yet Cliff. You see, at a funeral you can't leap on a woman and tug at her hair to find out. Maybe it's not a wig. Maybe dyed. Maybe it's not Rosie Dunn. Except she's wearing Rosie's ring.'

'But you think so?'

'I'm not one hundred per cent sure. Yes, she's alive. But I've got to see, Cliff, with my own eyes. I need to know why. That's what it's about, Cliff. When I know, Ruth Dunn will come clean. She won't have any choice. And Charlie Dunn will get his money's worth, one way or another.'

'Mum sends her love,' said Cliff and picked up another scone. 'She wants to know if we'll go over Sunday night for dinner.'

Sophie sighed quietly. Cliff would sit in front of the tele after the baked dinner while Mrs Cray and Sophie did the dishes and Mrs Cray went over Cliffie's faults, as if they were the main bargaining point in the matrimonial stakes. Then Mr Cray would come in for a tongue bashing and they'd still be in the kitchen having a sherry while the ·boys got stuck into the beer.

'I'm not having a bloody record of the Baskerville hounds baying.' Sophie wandered around the house to take in the security devices.

'They're dobermans,' replied literal Cliff. 'George reckons they'd frighten the shit out of anyone.'

Cliff had taken down the slashed Brett Whiteley. 'George's got a mate who does restoring of painting. Used to be in the business,' Cliffie had a snigger, 'in Europe. Still does a few jobs.'

'Forger,' thought Sophie but didn't enquire. Cliff didn't believe in sharing sordid details with his lady friend.

Sophie returned to the kitchen and waved to George with his thick black curly hair and a dreadlock over the right ear. His mate smiled too. He was dreadlocked fore and aft.

'I just wish,' Cliff buttered Sophie another scone, 'that you'd get into something feminine like . . .'

'A lingerie saleswoman?' asked Sophie, temper flaring.

'Come on, Soph, you know what I mean. Maybe antiques or a little restaurant.'

The telephone rang. It was Jamey boy, breathless and pleased with himself.

'They're down at Camp Cove. The house is owned by a woman called Elise Cadogan. She's been there off and on for eighteen months. There isn't any Mr Cadogan, but now and then a gentleman calls. I've got his numberplate.'

'Good,' Sophie noted down the name. 'Just watch, Jamey.'

'That's easy. There's only one way out from the street. I'm parked around the corner.'

'Where did you get the information?'

'Corner shop. Chatty old bloke. Been there forever.'

'You'll be relieved at six.'

'OK,' said Jamey boy, resigned. 'I'll do a bit of reading.'

'Let's go,' said Sophie to Cliff, hanging up.

'Where to?' Cliff pulled on his leather jacket.

'To the Gap. I want to commune.'

She and Cliff got into her car and they were silent until the Bondi bypass. Then Sophie said, 'They're not running yet, Cliff. They're still playing the game. Maybe Jim Stokes was a double agent. Maybe doubling on the drugs side. Maybe not. But someone killed him, so someone knew Jim Stokes would meet me. Had someone decided to kill him anyway, Cliff, and used the situation to warn me off as well?'

'Maybe,' Cliff looked glum. 'Maybe it was a convenient place. I mean, he wouldn't know what you looked like. You only spoke by phone.'

'Yes, but for the meantime we are safe. You see, we're not in this to break into the business or expose it, Cliff.' Half the journos in Sydney would love a big bust book with names named and operations traced, she thought. Half of the politicians were busy shredding the reputations of the other half. New Royal Commissions were planned on vice and crime.

They pulled into the kerb.

'I hate this bloody place,' Cliff said as he helped her over the fence and took her hand.

Sophie glanced at the road. The scenario had changed for her now. A car had come there late at night. Probably at two or three, when the road would be deserted. A headless body had been pulled from the boot and carried along the path ahead.

Soph sat well back from the edge while Cliffie did his macho bit, sauntering around the ledge and waiting for Sophie to protest.

The sea was ahead, stretching out. Far out were the circling gulls blown like scraps of paper against the grey clouds. The horizon promised no new land. Only itself, always further. Rosie Dunn would never have come here by herself. Rosie wouldn't like the distance of sky and sea, which was always changing but offering no real solace for a suburban girl.

But then, Rosie Dunn wasn't like that, she remembered. Rosie might well have stood at the edge, confident, arrogant, certain.

Sophie took herself back to the funeral – Ruth Dunn turning around to see who was there. She had to. Any woman would do the same. Ruth Dunn had concentrated heavily on her entry – the dignity, the composed face, the unfaltering step. She would have gone past the guests at the funeral rites, unseeing. Staring maybe at the gold cross on the altar, the unlit candles, the window above with Christ, as usual, suffering a bad case of terminal depression.

Then she would return to herself as Ruth Dunn, the woman, and want to know if the church was full or half empty. Whether many of Rosie's friends had come. How many of the family had put in an appearance. What the place looked like, which all together confirmed that destiny had been at work in the Dunn household and what happened to the other families happened to hers.

And the look had frozen and Ruth Dunn had forgotten her curiosity and had hurriedly, like someone witnessing an obscenity, turned back, straight and proud, the Eastern suburbs matron who did not notice what didn't fit into her world.

So Rosie Dunn had been there. Just as Rosie Dunn might have stood here with Rufus Stone. With the waves leaping in sensual frenzy at the land.

What was the attraction of Rosie for Rufus Stone? For therein lay the mystery of Rosie Dunn. Was Rosie Dunn the ultimate tinsel girl? The false Duessa that Sydney had thrown up? What attracted Rufus Stone?

Sophie asked the question out loud and Cliffie shuffled. 'It can't just be the boy, one generation from the wrong side of the tracks, meeting girl always on the right side?'

❖ ❖ ❖

Cliffie was still peeved as they strolled along Macleay Street at the Cross. The main drag was beginning to wind up for its evening business. Tits would be swinging in the strip joints, blue films churning out ten thousand similar lusts as someone groaned, moaned and simulated coming. The glitter glatter boys were on the pavement selling.

'You know,' said Cliff, 'I used to know an old Belgium lady who made the ladies' noises in the blue films. She reckoned she was good at it because she used to sing opera when she was young. Gave her vocal range and stamina.'

'How about it, lady?' asked one of the glitter glatter boys. Cliff had fallen back to look in a pawnshop window. 'Male strippers. Real turn-ons and beautiful and big where the ladies like taking a peek.'

Rosie Dunn had walked along this pavement many, many times, wending her way past potential slashers and the nut cases on their prescription drugs. Around at the Wayside Chapel, with the moon almost at the full, the phones would be ringing red hot as the waves were thrown up against the rocks at the Gap. Kids would have visions, men would beat their wives, drunks would forget the gas, and Rosie Dunn, somewhere in the city, would dream as Elise Cadogan?

'What are we going to do now, Soph?' They were standing outside Janet Craig's place. The plants were as dismal as ever. The lamp-post waiting for someone to lean against it.

'We're going to the opera, Cliff. Down at the Domain. And we'll take a bottle of wine and some chicken.'

Sophie led Cliff back up to the car, 'You know Cliff, we've not really had a summer this year.'

❖ 13 ❖

The sky was still eggshell blue with hints of white. More like a distant idea of winter that would happen somewhere else. Like New Zealand in the South, where the trees turned scarlet and the air was like lettuce out of the crisper – green, fresh and dying.

Here, the sky-scrapers were isolated on the sky like drawings of geometry figures. Behind Sophie, the Cahill Expressway continued to deliver its burden of cars to the Harbour Bridge, and to the left the Art Gallery hoisted its façade into prominence like a Manchester businessman suffering delusions of grandeur.

The stage was smallish, and high towers held the sound equipment needed since eighty thousand people were lounging around on an evening that was as warm as the opera was late. Dame Joan suffering tonsilitis perhaps?

Sophie decided she would consult on that with Sophia Mavrakis, somewhere here. Pity, too, there wasn't a librettist since most of the characters of the Rosie Dunn story would be here. Sophie picked her way through the throng. Somewhere Sophia would be sitting with friends, primed up on sweet champagne.

Norma, as planned, had reserved space with a large mohair rug. Jamey boy sat beside her looking at a polaroid photo of Henri the Kanak Basher. Henri had been snapped in the wherewithal, showing the show. The dangers, thought

Sophie with a sigh, of modern technology.

'He looks very nice,' offered Jamey politely. Norma arched an eyebrow, sighed once or twice and confessed to a similar reaction.

'Lo, Norma, Jamey.' Sophie sat herself down with Cliff. Norma was in a long cream silk casual kaftan. Sophie, as Norma took note, was wearing crumpled jeans.

'How's Henri?' asked Sophie.

'Left this morning for New Caledonia. I'm sure one of those Kanak's going to give him the chop. If he gets back he's decided on Sydney for his future, retail business and restaurant. Might find myself behind the cash register before long. Henri thinks I've got the right kinda personality for the job. Henri will cook. He's got a Cordon Bleu diploma. Did it one summer in Paris.'

'All a bit casual here, isn't it, Soph?' Norma stood up to take in the green sward and the umbrellas. 'Half the queens of Sydney have turned up,' announced Norma loudly to those around.

'Come off it, Norma,' Cliff admired the photo of Henri. 'That's no way to talk about people at an event. Anyway, how do you know what people do or don't do in bed?'

'I've had plenty of experience,' Norma took the photo back. 'Particularly after my lesbian affair with Romana. Henri says, too, that a fling on the side never hurt anyone.'

'Bloody frogs!' Cliffie turned moody.

Norma offered garlic chicken pieces, bread, wine, pâté and a potato salad. Sophie took some chicken and salad. The lights went up on the front as the sun declined into a red light matched by that lighting the Art Gallery façade.

'He's arrived,' announced Norma to the claps and boos.

'Who?' asked Sophie.

'Mr Hawke. *The Prime Minister*,' Norma added, in case anyone might have missed the change in government a million years ago.

The orchestra struck up 'Advance Australia Fair'. The beach umbrellas came down. Sophie got to her feet as she liked a good sing along: 'Deutschland Über Alles', 'The People's Flag' or 'God Save the Queen'.

Cliffie glowered at a few non-Nationalists, a group of Poms with no respect and still guzzling at quiche and handing around a joint. A couple of the ladies were embracing. Norma looked interested.

'Like dried blood,' Jamey pointed at the Art Gallery.

Norma put down her glass. 'I'm off to the loo before Our Joanie hitches up her skirts and gets stuck in.'

Half the audience thought the same. The queues, Sophie noted through her binoculars, were stretching forever. The police were there, at the far end, away from the trysting place with Sophia Mavrakis. Also an ambulance. For a moment Sophie thought she caught sight of the bleached blonde hair, a slight weasel-shaped body standing by a tree, then the shadow moved and that was that.

She sat down again, counted her pulse and waited. The first tale ended with moderate applause; more being saved for the Diva. Then Dame Joan Sutherland was on and Sophie was moving out at an arc as the soaring voice caught into the stars and the audience fused into a single creature. Not letting herself go as much as she used to. Pacing, thought Sophie. Holding everything for the right moment.

Ahead, in the gloom, were the blue lavatories, and, as Sophia Mavrakis had prophesied, behind her the collective sphincter was easily holding as the collective soul floated up into the sky where the animal couldn't go.

A whiff of disinfectant brought Sophie back to herself. She tilted her Peruvian shopping bag, felt the handle of the Biretta, grasped it and walked on. Then began running, since through the orchestra and song she could hear something like feet drumming against corrugated iron. Like a stage rainstorm, or thunder at the school play.

Cliffie saw her and ran too, and like two sides of the bow they arrived stretched taut.

Ahead was the end loo, and the door was half-shut like the rest. Sophie stood for a moment waiting for the stage witch to announce herself with a low chuckle.

Then the drumming, now fainter, started again as Dame Joan began the 'Doll' aria.

Sophie pushed against the door and felt something give. She took out her torch and saw two spindly varicosed legs waving in the air, a pair of nylon undies frilled with fake lace, a section of lower white back and a rucked-up black chenille dress.

Gagging, Cliff did the man's work, boot against the tin, hands around the waist. The lid cracked and the seat disintegrated as Sophia Mavrakis reappeared, blonde wig primped and set for the big occasion, powdered dripping face, thin weasel lips in a rictus of horror that relaxed and took breath.

The mouth opened wider and poured out a series of profound obscenities.

Sophia Mavrakis then vomited, wept and sat up and clasped at her leaking handbag. She opened it and emptied it on to the grass.

Sophie handed over her silver flask. Sophia Mavrakis gasped, drank and held the brandy down.

'Stomach pump,' suggested Sophie. 'Hospital?'

'Little bitch,' screeched Sophia Mavrakis. 'Don't think it wasn't her and her mates. Didn't get me bloody bag, though!'

'Who?'

Sophia clamped her lips shut.

'Have you friends here?' asked Sophie.

The mouth opened. 'Yer, sure. And do you think they are gunna see me like this?'

Sophie shone her torch into the lavatory. On the floor was the calling card. She picked it up. It was her licence to Private Dickery Dock.

'She could have died,' said Cliff to Sophie.

'No deal now,' rasped Sophia finishing off the brandy. Sophie took back the flask, found a piece of paper, wrapped it and put it in her bag.

Sophia Mavrakis looked around. 'Do me a favour and take me home. Me friends mustn't see what that bitch and her friends did.'

'Friends?'

'How do I know? But I heard the bitch laugh. Didn't see

anything. Bloody amazing. Bloody cops hundred yards off. But I remember that bloody laugh.'

'What did Rosie Dunn want from you, Sophia? Was it a body? There you are down at the Cross, lots of connections. A morgue attendant maybe? Or just someone who checks the streets and finds the overdosed? Did she want a body Sophia, to go over the Gap?'

'No comment,' said Sophia, lips tight. 'No comment. Only one thing. Your bloody phone must be tapped. How otherwise did they know!'

❖ ❖ ❖

Back at home the phone rang. Sophie picked it up, switched on record. She heard coins dropping and waited. 'Hi, Soph,' said Mike, the tail. 'I lost the tart at the Opera.'

'I know, Mike. Was she alone?'

'Na. With a guy.'

'What now?'

'Went back to the house. Then left again.'

'Did you follow?'

'Yer, sure thing, Soph. That's where I am now. The airport.'

'Where are they going, Mike?'

'Got up to the flight desk,' Mike's voice held a touch of self esteem. 'She's on her way to Thailand. Flight leaves at one. He didn't see her off. Dropped her then drove away. Made sure he stopped along from the main doors, too. Secretive bastard.'

'With reason, Mike.'

'OK. Do I go back to the house at Camp Cove?'

'No, cut the shift short. I'll call you if I need more work.'

'OK. Give me best to Cliff.'

'Will do.' Sophie hung up.

❖ 14 ❖

It had been a risk. She knew that from the moment she got on the plane, Cliffie trailing behind her with his new Qantas bag and a bad case of nerves.

It had been a risk going through the customs in Bangkok and a greater risk spending a couple of days at Hotel Miami. Outside the glass doors had been the crooks the notice warned against. The crooks had had a fine old time with Cliffie. 'You wanna live sex show five hundred *bhat*, then massage and girl extras? You wanna boy?' Despairingly, 'Maybe you wan something special. You tell?'

'Australian parrot,' had said Cliff curtly. 'I want an Australian parrot.' The oriental Buddhist crooks looked at the pavement and considered bad karma and the round of creation, the wheel and other esoteric matters. 'You wanna girl?' they tried again.

The bus ride down to the South had been uneventful. One army search with those thin-faced, acid and angry soldiers on lethal short fuses. The Thais cowered. Sophie smiled gently, as a *farang*. Pleased too she was unarmed, though her finger itched for the Biretta. Just in case. Just in case the game was about to turn rough, down in Phuket.

It was there that Rosie Dunn must be. It was where her old Thai boyfriend 'Good' Luk had set up bungalows.

Rosie Dunn would be somewhere about, laughing a little at the events of the last week. Her funeral in particular.

And now, safe away before the hounds closed in.

Rosie's flat, down at the Cross, had been broken into. Charlie Dunn had rung to tell her, voice booming hostility for the criminal who had blown a wall safe in the sitting room. Charlie however couldn't think what of value might have been in it. It was more the principle. 'Druggies,' Charlie Dunn had growled. 'No respect for private property.'

Charlie was also in the news. He'd performed three coronary by-passes on a Federal senator.

Sophia Mavrakis had hit the tabloids. She had been taken to St Vincent's Hospital, her stomach pumped out and put on a twenty-four-hour antibiotic drip.

Someone had leaked her to the journos. They were around like festive dingoes. Sophia had given a news conference and blasted evil powers, posed against the backdrop of Byzantine saints holding her crystal globe. The wig had obviously been dry-cleaned and reset for the photo. Sophia, however, had not vouchsafed any particulars of who her persecutors might be. Equally, she had no answer as to why her clairvoyance hadn't picked up 'her baptism', as one paper had coyly called it, 'in the lower effects of opera enthusiasm'.

Cliffie had re-read the article, sniggered, taken a sleeping pill and slept for the remainder of the trip.

❖ ❖ ❖

At Phuket she'd taken a taxi, Cliffie following on in a hired motorbike. Seeming separate might be more useful in an emergency. And, Happy Hour Bungalows at Kata Beach did indeed exist, even if the bus station touts claimed a score of other places were cheaper and friendlier.

The following evening Sophie left number three bungalow – double bed, mosquito net, fan, adjoining shower, a squat loo and local fauna – and put on her sunglasses. She was wearing a flash raw-silk number run up in Bangkok.

Allan the Pom out of Griffith, Australia, took a look and his rubbery lips opened into a welcoming smile. Cliff, sitting beside him, looked a mite embarrassed, but that was expected.

Cliff had been down at Madame Tui's on his first night, and for authenticity had picked up a girl. Cliff was to ask a bit about the foreign women around the place. Nothing too direct.

The cast was still gathering and the sun lowering. Across the paddy fields, burned and dry, a solitary water buffalo plodded. Luk was playing his guitar.

A jeep swept off the road, scattering homeward-bound chooks and with a clash of gears halted three feet from one of the pigs.

Conan leapt from the jeep followed at a leisurely pace by the former French junkie queen. The lady had only recently transferred her affections and Conan had already filled Sophie in on the former scene. 'Her "ex" overdosed, man. Like he woke up dead in Bombay and she, my chick, was lying beside him waiting for the day to get goin. He liked screwin in the morning. So. Good shock therapy, man. She keepin herself better now, only cocaine and some pills.'

'Hi, Sophie, you have good day?' enquired Conan. Sophie eyed the bleached blond hair, the feral face, white teeth and blue splintered eyes, the green bead necklace at the throat, the t-shirt with Superbeast written in arterial red. Where had she been all these years? There was a definite stirring in the lower abdomen.

'Wanta drink?' asked Conan, striding the last few feet to the table.

'I'll shout.' Sophie went to the bar and Conan looked puzzled.

'What you mean, "shout"?'

'Drinks,' Sophie threw back over her shoulder.

'Bloody mad Ozzies! Shout for drinks!' Conan cupped his hands around his mouth and shouted.

Luk, behind the bar, smiled and took down the gin bottle.

'Where's Jose-Maria?' asked Sophie.

'Mary?' Conan grinned. 'He's just on his way, man. Any moment now.'

'I wouldn't mind just settling here.' Cliff sipped on his beer and addressed himself to Conan. 'Must be a few people around doing that. Dunno how they manage for visas.'

'Easy man. You bribe Police Chief, or you bribe customs. Just go down to Malaysia for the day.'

'Many doing it, you know, staying around here?'

'Few man. Just a few permanents. Most is moving group. Here, up to India, over to Sri Lanka. Plenty of things to do.'

Sophie imagined.

Rosie Dunn, wherever she was, knew Luk. And Conan and Jose-Maria had been around Phuket for three years off and on. They'd known Luk that long. Ergo, Rosie Dunn?

'Me,' said Cliff to Conan, in reply to something Sophie hadn't listened to, 'I like blondes best. I'd get kinda tired of bar girls. Used to know a couple of girls who came up here. We all studied at university together. Anthropology. Then one of them croaked. She was blonde, called Rosie Dunn. Real high-class kid.'

Sophie glanced quickly at Conan's face. The flint eyes might have shadowed slightly but the red lips didn't move. Allan, however, looked down at his drink then started playing with the domino counters.

Conan put his arm around Cliff's shoulders.

'Conan takes downers,' said the former junkie queen to Sophie, 'and he just speeds up. I mean he vibrates at ten times the rate of everyone else. I just don't know how he doesn't shatter. Man!' She looked at the approaching rooster with his hens. 'It's a tiring thing changing men.'

With a burn of dust, a clash of gears and a large jeep, Mary arrived, his heavy gut flopping over his denims, t-shirt loudly proclaiming 'Beat Me, Bite Me, Suck Me, Fuck Me'.

Mary, so Sophie already knew via Allan, had inherited a cool million dollars from his father. Mary had then run away from his mother, a cocaine queen who pinched his fixes. Mary had gone through 700,000 dollars and was heading for a fast obituary.

Sophie smiled at Jose-Maria – a motherly, warm smile.

'Goin to Madame Tui's tonight?' Allan asked Cliff.

Cliff shrugged. Allan gave a broad wink. Jose-Marie

belched. Like the gong in Metro Goldwyn Mayer, it announced his attention to entertainment.

The French Embassy couple smiled from their table and stuck to their own company. Sophie herself was starting to feel frazzled.

There was tension here and tonight Cliff would show the picture of Rosie Dunn. Not in public, not under those Xmas tree lights that framed Tui's honey trap with its wooden tables, concrete dance patch and lots of girls sitting around, bored, tourism falling off as the monsoon approached. No, Cliff was smart and had picked out an older bar girl, one who spoke quite good American from the R and R days and had been around this small patch of beach for five or six years, according to Luk when Cliffie had asked about her this morning. Tonight Cliff would roll on his rubber, perform, and in the post-operative glow produce the picture of Rosie Dunn and ask.

And now with the sun gone and the mosquitoes homing in, Sophie was taking Allan down to the beach shack restaurants for a bite to eat. Allan was giving her a loving eye. Understandable. Allan had fled Oz on a British passport, warned off by the cops and deserting fame and fortune, not to mention fifty acres near Griffith spread about with marijuana.

Allan was living on Luk's charity and washing a few dishes while he waited for money owed. The daughter in Brixton was sending a loan soon. Allan had rung.

Allan, with fifty dollars tucked into his pocket, might talk. Less risky than Luk, inscrutable happy Luk. 'Good' Luk. Part Chinese, part Thai. Songs and songs he had: Bobby Dylan, The Jackson Five, The Rolling Stones, The Beatles. Luk had his book with the words copied out and the chord changes. Luk played every night with poetry swimming in his eyes as he watched the till.

'Ja, well, tonight we go to Thai boxing,' said Conan. 'Why not you come, Sophie? Allan come, Mary come, my woman come. We go in jeep. In Phuket town. Really good show. They beat shit out of each other. Broken teeth and jaws and howl like mad, but when leave ring, very dignified like Buddhist monk. All passion, you see, is just dream.'

'And broken teeth and jaws?' asked Sophie.

'Also dream,' decided Conan the Barbarian, 'just kharma and plenty of money. They live real good those boxer boys. Blood is all chicken blood. They have in mouth then break the plastic. Have specially filed back teeth. And broken bones is just fake.

'You know, people here is very simple. They don't mind illusion; since everything is illusion, why not a bit more? Don't need American reality. You know, real broken bones and maybe a nice murder to cheer them up.

'Schopenhauer,' said Cliffie unexpectedly, 'Schopenhauer was into all that.'

Conan the Barbarian turned Germanic and respectful. 'You read Schopenhauer, man?'

'Yer,' Cliff lied valiantly. 'Kinda like his ideas.'

'So,' belched Mary, 'we meet up here at nine o'clock. Boxing at ten, then we go back to my place. My old Mama San cook real good. I ring her now with menu for tonight.'

'No funny business, Mary,' said Conan looking significantly at Sophie. 'We have ladies with us so no funny business and no girls.'

'OK, OK, no funny business.' Mary ambled over to the phone, purposeful and ready for extended hospitality.

Conan and the junkie queen took off for destination unknown.

The French couple relaxed and invited Sophie in French to sit at their table.

Cliffie wandered off to his bungalow for a catch-up snooze.

Allan went over to the darts board and threw a few twenties.

◆ ◆ ◆

It was a soft, easy walk to the beach. The dust road was easy and the smiling faces of the houseboys at Kata bungalows easy. This was the short cut – through the manicured flowerbeds and out on to the beach with ahead the ocean, framed by the headland and the palms and then the sand warm and soft, the other headland making a crescent for the water.

The moon was there, full and bright.

They wended their way past the fishing boats, prows high on the sand.

'The best food,' said Allan diplomatically, 'is the third shack along.'

Omo, the fat-faced owner, brought glasses with a smile and patted Allan on the back for coming home first, for a change.

Sophie produced her bottle of duty-free cognac.

'So what happened back in Griffith?' Sophie asked after the second convivial drink.

'Dobbed in.' Allan patted boss Dog, on the lookout for scraps. 'Cops were OK. Said I had twenty-four hours before they'd make an arrest. I ditched me Australian passport and went out on the Brit. one. Lost a lot of money. All me money, though I still own the land with me partner.'

'Where is the farm?'

'Well, that would be telling.'

Sophie looked up at the headland with the Somerset Maugham house. Wooden, low-slung, colonial style. The sort of place where a writer or lover of Marlowe could brood happily over the sea, the moonlit sea, the sea of truth and eternity, gentler than the sea at the Gap. The same water and ocean, but tamed by place and, said her practical persona, a long gentle plateau of rock leading up to this bay.

'What are you doin here, Sophie?' Allan took one of her Benson and Hedges; the Gauloise had proved too tough for the throat.

Sophie smiled at Omo, arriving with the stir-fried prawns, the rice and vegies. And a bottle of beer.

She ate.

Allan ate.

They quietly digested and took in paradise again.

'I mean,' said Allan, 'it's so bloody perfect. They don't

care about time. Don't care about progress. They just, kinda, exist. I mean, who would need to invest anything when it just falls outa a tree.'

'What?' asked Sophie.

'It's all here. Food, fish, booze, women, kindness. They're really kind. They don't have that kinda English thing of the future. I've lost it quite a bit, too. When the money comes in I'll buy in here and just stay. Why go some place else? No point. No point. I'll settle down.'

'Marvellous.' Sophie looked at Allan. That large brown face and those large blue shifty eyes; like an owl in daylight. Those lines of ease which were also of acquiescence. Sophie put the photo of Rosie Dunn on the table. 'Take a look, Allan. I think you know her.'

Allan took the photo. Then he stopped looking and stared at the dribble of beer in the bottom of the glass and then looked up at the house, the Somerset Maugham house, the romantic house, just above them on the headland.

'Thank you, Allan.' Sophie took back the photo.

Then she reached into her bag and brought out a fifty-dollar note. Allan took it and looked at it.

'They said in Sydney she was dead.'

Allan listened.

'She was my cousin. She remains "was", Allan, but I want to know.'

'Funny,' Allan swilled out the beer dregs.

'Find out any gossip Allan.'

'Yeah,' Allan looked down at his empty plate. 'Dunno if I can. I dunno.'

'You can. Just listen. No problems.'

'You narcotics, Sophie?'

Sophie shook her head. 'Get me some information and there'll be another fifty.'

'Yeah well.' Allan looked along the beach. 'It's time to go for the boxing.'

❖ ❖ ❖

It was in a large hall off the colonial-style main square. The crowds were jostling but Conan the Barbarian pushed through and disappeared in a side door. Minutes later he reappeared, a fat smile on his face, waving the tickets.

'OK,' Mary looked beneficent, 'the show's on me.' Mary shoved a wad of *bhats* into Conan's jacket pocket. 'Let's go, man.' Mary led the way, and the party followed in his waddling wake.

Inside, the hall was thick with smoke and Thais. Sophie lit up herself as they sat in prime ringside seats. Conan handed around some lines of cocaine from Mary. Sophie sniffed and floated. Reminded her a bit of the first race at Randwick with the week's housekeeping on an outsider to win.

'High grade,' Conan sniffed. 'Real high grade coke.'

The ex-heroin queen lit up a reefer, adjusted her headphones and sat back and smiled at a couple of friendly policemen.

'No problems for us,' said Mary to Sophie. 'We know them all. They come for parties, girls and to snort. We well in with Big Boys of Phuket. No problems.'

Allan sniffed too, his large owl eyes steadier. Sophie bought some beers and handed them along.

The warm-up boxers came on.

'High as kites,' said the ex-heroin queen. 'Won't feel a thing!'

Sophie felt herself drifting up around cloud eight. Conan gave her a companionable squeeze on the thigh.

'Jesus,' shouted Conan letting go. 'Right in the teeth, man. Look at that.'

Sophie looked. A diminutive Thai was on his knees moaning, blood pouring from his mouth and what looked like a couple of teeth through his lips. The Thai victor aimed a kick at his opponent's neck and what sounded like a chicken having its neck broken snapped Sophie back into reality.

'Great.' Sophie declined another line of cocaine and stopped thinking about the smell of vomit. Concentrated on Rosie Dunn, who was coming into focus again, like a kind of emptiness that washed away the boxers, the next round, the next fight, the fight after that and the pushing and shoving out into the steaming air of Phuket town.

She came down at Mary's house, a white effort with a browned-up garden and a few strands of flowering bougainvillea.

'So welcome.' Mary struck a boxer's pose of victory. 'Now we eat!'

Sophie smelled the food.

'She real good cook, this old Mama San.' Mary sat down on the floor and reached for the box where the goodies were stored. 'Tonight it's Chinese. Duck in mushroom sauce, fried rice, pan-fried vegetables, sweet and sour pork and some lychees.'

'Oh boy.' Conan licked his chops and nuzzled the junkie queen. 'I love sweet and sour pork. My sister made sweet and sour for me. Now she marry to a merchant in carpets and lives in big villa outside Munich. She always love her brother best, though. She give me whatever I want.'

'She,' asked Mary, 'the one you used to screw with?'

'Ja, when kids we screw like mad, now we just friends.'

Sophie felt her bog Catholic hackles coming up.

The food arrived. Duck in lemon sauce and almonds, no sweet and sour but a soup followed by stir-fried fish.

Mary sat next to her and patted her and encouraged her to eat like he ate – on and on and on. Mary smacked his lips, handed around the whisky and ordered the junkie queen to push in a tape.

'*Chariots of Fire*,' announced Mary. 'I really like that music. Cruddy story though, like a loada boy scouts!'

The bong was lit and Sophie took a drag and handed it on, lay back on the cushions and felt the roof fan blowing waves of air over her.

Someone changed the tape and Cleo Laine came on, then someone else and Conan saying, 'Now, Mary, you keep your hands off that big dame. She real nice and she not like big fat boys fumbling with her underpants.'

Conan sounded tough.

Mary giggled.

'Now you play guard Allan,' ordered Conan. 'Me and my lady is off for a screw. OK Allan?'

'OK,' Allan replied.

Conan left. The heroin queen bent down and gave Mary a long, loving kiss. In her world, guessed Sophie, you never knew when it might be time to move on again.

Sophie half-opened her eyes. Mary was half-lying, supported by large cushions. Allan was in the cane rocking-chair flipping through a magazine.

Mama San arrived with more tea. Sophie came awake, drank, the bitter taste clearing her brain. The ploy had worked. People passed out in Mary's house probably for days at a time.

Mary eyed her with a large smile.

'It's a great place,' Sophie said. 'You must meet a lot of people being a Big Guy around town.'

'Yeah.' Mary look gratified.

Sophie double-checked the feeling of Mary. No need for any preliminaries.

She got up, changed the cassette back to Cleo Laine – *Gymnopédies* of Satie. Melodies for a child taking his first step, a girl reading by herself in a room with the rain beating against the window.

Mary relaxed into being himself. Sophie lowered herself down on to the cushions beside him and softly, like a mother, cradled Mary's head against her breasts. Mary's lips puckered as if he wouldn't mind taking a late-night suck.

'Funny how life is,' said Mary. 'You just go on but it change. Look different. Ain't the same life as when you was little.' Sophie stroked his greasy black hair and felt for a moment a surprising tug at her lachrymose glands. 'Things happen and you dunno why. You know why, Sophie?'

'I knew someone like that,' Sophie smiled at Allan in his chair perving at the centrefold of *Playboy*. 'A young girl with blonde hair and innocence. Then a worm got in. She got into drugs and something happened to her.'

'Jesus,' said Mary. 'Just like me. It's like a dream. But that's all it is anyway, according to the monks here. Justa dream.'

'She might have been murdered, she might have suicided. But she won't even be remembered in eighty years' time. That's how it is Mary, not remembered. Just like us.'

'Si,' Mary snuggled.

Sophie felt in her pockets for the second battered copy of the photo of Rosie Dunn.

'This is what she looked like. She was a beautiful girl.'

Mary, who admired blondes, took the photo and studied it.

'She's dead, Mary. She went off the Gap in Sydney. It's a kind of Lovers' Leap. It's a very high cliff and way down the sea and rocks.'

Mary chuckled to himself. 'She look like someone I know. Seen her around, that girl.'

'She's dead. I went to her memorial service a while back.'

Mary chuckled again and finally sat up to wheeze out some laughter like a blocked-up bellows. 'Christ! Fuck Me! Life's funny!'

Sophie stroked Mary's hair.

Allan put down the magazine and stared at a large painting of Marilyn Monroe showing more than she should. Allan's eyes were large and round like his face, and they showed fear.

'I reckon we should go,' said Allan. 'That girl's dead, you know. Better off forgetting it all.'

'Bullsheet!' said Mary, his large olive face crinkling like a spoilt child who didn't like being contradicted. His belly spilling over his open shirt, tightened with the memory of muscle that had been there once.

'Let's go, Sophie.' Allan stood up. 'He gets violent in some moods.'

'Bullsheet!' screetched Mary, face growing redder. He flopped back on the cushions. 'Anyway, I've gotta sleep and think. I want some sun and sea tomorrow. But she's hanging around in my skull, that girl. I've just gotta sleep and think then I'll remember where I've put her and it ain't in the RIP section. She's there somewhere. Oh man, yes, she's there.'

'Go and order a taxi, Allan.'

101

Allan nodded to Sophie, pleased to be ordered around.

'Now,' said Sophie to Mary, 'we're alone together.'

Mary liked that line and tried to snuggle.

'Why don't we meet and talk about that lovely girl,' suggested Sophie, soft, maternal.

'OK,' Mary snuggled. 'I like you. We meet. Tomorrow night.' Mary yawned and went foetal. 'Full moon party at Omo's tomorrow night. Across paddy fields from Happy Hour.'

'Why don't you come down on the beach. We can talk down there, privately, since tomorrow you'll remember all about Rosie Dunn.'

'Who's Rosie Dunn?' asked Mary.

'The girl in the photo.'

'Yer, a nice name. Rosita. Kinda homey. Yer, I remember in morning.'

'So we meet around ten thirty tomorrow night, down at the creek, at the end. Nice and quiet there.'

'Yer,' Mary yawned like a baby. 'Si. Nice walk.'

Sophie found a wrap and tucked him in. Mary yawned again.

Sophie left.

Outside Allan was standing with the *samlor* primed to go. They got in. They passed the town brothel.

'No better than India,' Allan offered. 'They reckon there are fifty women in there. Most of 'em on smack. Some, they reckon, are chained to their beds. All sorts of nasty rumours. The Thais don't like it but they reckon the District Governor's got shares.'

Allan was sweating. Sophie knew why. Allan was trying to decide what he should do. Should he talk to someone. His large blue eyes looked down at his large fat hands.

'Going to talk, Allan?' asked Sophie.

Allan looked defensive. 'I'm no grass.'

They arrived at Happy Hour bungalows. Sophie walked up the steps. Luk was up, guitar on his lap. Somewhere, like an egg beater, a loud egg beater, a change was being announced. Sophie took out Rosie Dunn's photo and ordered a small beer.

'Janet Craig told me you'd talk about Rosie, my cousin. I want to know what happened.'

Luk put aside his guitar and studied Rosie.

The noise was getting louder.

Allan went to his bungalow.

Somewhere Cliff, in his own bungalow or at his lady's place, would be listening too. Suddenly, she hoped Cliff had got what he needed to know and sent the lady packing. Somehow tonight, Sophie needed Clifford Cray.

The helicopter was now arriving.

It swung in close and she saw its markings and then it disappeared in an arch that took it to the headland. A moment later it had landed and a moment after that the motor was cut.

Luk smiled at Sophie. 'So you ask me about your cousin, Rosie? Rosie find way to make white light into many colours. She live in this. Maybe like queen of old times, Rosie Dunn believes in power and strength.'

'And you?'

Luk shrugged and played more chords, listening intently to his sound. 'I am Buddhist. I believe in many things different from you.

'I believe some beings are caught in lusts and go to hells. Some are pure beings like Buddha and give compassion to them. Some beings are creative and on a journey, and Rosie Dunn went on a journey. Already prepared, Sophie, in her karma.' Luk played more. It sounded a bit like Debussy. 'Sad songs, happy songs, ending songs. Rosie Dunn sing them all and then new songs.'

'Who was the man who broke up the white light?'

'The Big Man? Not me, Sophie. I am just beginning of song. The Big Man is also boy. Who want second life, like Rosie Dunn. A life where there is also adventure and danger and where you make a story.'

'And now?'

Luk smoothed down his perfumed hair. 'It is like a story for Rosie. You say "kill" and person dies. You say "give me", it is given.'

'Do you know the past tense in English, Luk?' Sophie turned over her hand and studied her palm. No breaks. No sudden accidents of death were written there.

'In English and Thai, me and Rosie Dunn always speak in present and sometimes future. Never past. This is my memory of Rosie Dunn.'

Luk put down the guitar and studied his own palms. 'I have long happy life. I make much money. I am third of ten children. A Taoist man tell me these things. He live in room in Bangkok. He flee from China and now sell vegetables and he is scholar and doesn't care. He tell me I have long life and make much money.

'My mother is Chinese woman and very pleased in this. She knows I will make the family strong again.

'Later, I go north to where village people have found things buried in the ground. Old tombs. Khmer tombs. I buy since I am almost first, for almost nothing. They don't know there is money for those things. I sell later to Americans for much money and I start travel business. Then I invest again and investment pay off down in Australia. So Rosie Dunn is very lucky for me. She call me "Good" Luk. So I am for her since then she find her man who is like her. She find her life and her journey.'

Sophie decided to play along. 'Why did Rosie Dunn decide to betray Rufus Stone. Why did she make it such a short journey?'

Luk shrugged. 'Maybe she forget she is just queen and must have king. Maybe she go into new room in herself and don't want no more. Difficult to know with Rosie Dunn. She never say what she feel. Rosie always watch and eyes like gems, don't show thought, just reflect light.'

'There were killings in Sydney after you left and Rosie Dunn died.'

Luk nodded. 'Some Thai men and Chinese men and some Australian men who think they can be independent. But not possible for king not allow. So they die. It is necessary when men are greedy.'

'It's late.' Sophie stood up. She had caught sight of Cliff

moving from his bungalow to hers and entering.

'Yes.' Luk played finishing chords. 'In week my little boy is home with us. Then I will be happy again.'

◆ ◆ ◆

Sophie entered her bungalow. Cliff, sitting on the bed, looked like a little boy about to be put on the mat.

'She bit,' said Cliff.

'Where?' asked Sophie with interest before catching on. She turned off her light, lit up a cigarette and watched the patch of lawn that led up to the restaurant and the room off the kitchen where Luk kept his safe and slept.

'She says that a woman like her was here. She says that she thinks she stays up at the house on the headland. She says she doesn't come down much to the beach. She also says the servants don't come from here and never talk about the house.'

Sophie raised her hand. Cliff shut himself off. A door creaked again. A moment later, Allan, wearing his sleeping sarong, came into view. He walked across and disappeared into Luk's room. They both heard what sounded like a flat palm connecting with someone's flesh.

Allan reappeared, rubbing his cheek. He stood looking around, shrugged and ambled off down the grassy slope. In Luk's room the light was turned off.

Sophie opened her door, motioned for her camera and set off to follow.

Cliff was beside her, holding a flashlight and what looked like a cosh.

They followed Allan's progress from palmtree to palmtree. He rounded the corner at Tui's honey trap.

Sophie and Cliff moved on to the road.

Cliff tugged at Sophie. 'He's going up to the big house.'

They found the track leading up to the headland. Cliff shone the flashlight ahead to check for snakes.

'What'll we see?' Cliff whispered.

They were now stationed with a clear view down on to the gravel drive.

'Destiny,' muttered Sophie, adjusting the telescopic lens. She checked through the infra-red vision finder and focused on the front door as Allan approached it and knocked. A guard came silently from the shadow of a tree, looked at him and nodded. Lights came on. The door opened. Allan moved backwards.

Framed perfectly in the doorway was Rufus Stone, and a moment later as the word was passed, Rosie Dunn. Rosie Dunn, Elise Cadogan, the woman at the Opera House, Janet's friend, was her natural blonde self.

Sophie clicked off another five shots. Then another three of the chopper, with Thai military markings on it. If that wasn't enough, the camouflage paint told the story.

❖ ❖ ❖

Afterwards, Sophie Parnell would half regret not stepping forward at that moment and calling cousin Rosie Dunn's bluff. But the sub-machine of the guard had dissuaded her, as had Rufus Stone's face and Rosie's Madonna-like expression. It was true what Luk said; Rosie Dunn showed nothing. That, too, dissuaded Sophie, as well as Cliff grabbing at her hand.

They had waited there for half an hour, long enough to cool; long enough to make their way safely down to the beach where Sophie sat watching the house up there with the lights on in what must be the sitting room. And where Rosie Dunn would look down from her eminence at the bathers, the pigs thrashing about, the dogs, the white sand, the crescent of headland.

Sophie muttered some verses to herself, jumbled up with death and destiny and Marlowe. *Festina lente, equi noctis.* Something like that, as Faustus waited for the chimes to strike twelve and the Devil to appear to claim his soul.

Cliff was quietly illumined, as if an epiphany had taken place up there.

'What is it Cliffie?' she asked, gentle, not wanting to intrude.

'I dunno. It's like we're watching a play, like life has a kind of pattern. Like watching someone about to fall.'

'Maybe, Cliff. That'll be Charlie Dunn's decision.'

They took off their clothes and ran into the water. They swam out steadily, and fifty yards offshore lay floating to watch the stars move slow into the destinies of man. The phosphorescence washed over Cliff in a swell from some distant steamer ploughing its way up the bight.

The helicopter took off again and arched out from the house. Rosie Dunn would be watching it, or Elise Cadogan would quietly go to bed, an aristocrat used to power, gracing country houses, old blood, the world a red carpet that rolled out before her until the end of time.

Sophie swam in slowly, recalling the Cross, the kids thieving, lying and dying. The scabs on them, the thinness that came over them as they walked the streets in their packs, living in someone's paid-up bedsit one week, in a squat the next or on a park bench. Finally, too ugly to sell their bodies, and finally, the last needle.

That was the truth, and Rosie Dunn was empress of their hell. It made what had to happen easier. It made it easier to tell Charlie Dunn. Rufus Stone, with his corruption and power, his magnetism, had shown the way, and empty Rosie Dunn had gratefully drunk of his life.

Cliff gave Sophie a kiss on the sand where the waves broke. They rolled around a bit.

'Always wanted to do that,' Cliff helped her up. 'Like *From Here to Eternity*.'

Sophie picked up some seaweed off herself.

'They'll kill us if they find out what we know,' said Cliff.

Sophie nodded. 'Only here . . . And they have to know we know . . . They don't. That's the ground rule, Cliff. Only necessary deaths. We are not yet necessary.'

She realised, later, the next night, that had she thought more, a necessary death was staring her in the face.

She didn't think though, and the next night she forgot as the French couple, she and Cliff walked through the gardens at Kata bungalows on their way to the restaurant.

She ate a pork fillet with cheese sauce while *Amadeus* came on the video, and was back in Vienna watching a genius who laughed in a high-pitched giggle. By the end, Cliffie had tears in his eyes while the horse-pulled hearse took the genius to a pauper's grave and quick lime.

'Let's walk,' suggested Philippe the attaché.

'Along the beach,' suggested Sophie, having provided her protection.

Sophie and Hélène took off their shoes and paddled along in the shallow water. The land crabs played fast games of touch football.

The moon cast shadows and far away over the paddy, Omo's party was in full cry. Ahead was the creek. Sophie glanced at her watch. Twenty minutes late, which didn't matter. Better in a way since she had her evidence.

'Jesus Christ!' Cliff pointed forward to where the stream debouched into the sea. It was low tide and a wide fan of wet sand was strewn with seaweed. Sophie forced herself to look, mainly because the cultural attaché had taken her arm and pulled her forward.

She felt her stomach turn over and she fell on her knees vomiting up the golden pork and accessories. Then she stood up and turned back to face what, after all, she must have caused.

Cliffie was standing lean and tall, his hair winnowed in the breeze, his face wide and vulnerable.

'*Merde,*' said the Ambassador's personal secretary. 'Do we just walk away?'

'Yes.' Sophie took her arm. 'We walked just a little way along and then sat and talked.'

'And then we went home,' said Cliff, beside her.

Sophie looked again. Mary, with his large olive face, had turned white like the underbelly of a fish. The land crabs had arrived but weren't worried about the face yet. It would soften when the body was brought back in on the next tide.

She concentrated on his eyes then on his lips. They and the tongue, bitten half-through, told the story. Mary, the fast kid, had earned a fast obituary. The guts, Sophie noted, were like a disembowelled cow. You couldn't call Mary a bull. Not even with what the sarong had exposed. But all those guts!

The stomach had been slashed three times, and Mary must have fallen and grabbed at them, held them and looked up at the face and the hands that held the machete.

Then he had let go his guts and they had flopped out and he had fallen on his back, felt the pain, bitten through his lips and tongue in his death agony, and had died.

'It looks like an abattoir,' said the cultural attaché. 'The colours are so pale.'

'Who is he?' asked the Ambassador's personal secretary. 'I have seen him up at Happy Hour.'

'We never saw it,' said the cultural attaché. 'We are on holidays, all of us. It must be drugs. Everything these days is drugs.'

'Yes,' said Sophie, walking away. 'Drugs. You're right – I think.'

. . . 'and that's how it was, Ruth. There he was with his tripes oozing around him and Rosie Dunn, up there on the headland, happy, at peace, so far above the world and its clamour. She finally came into focus, Ruth, and I understood.'

'You never intended to stop the investigation, did you?'

'No, Ruth.' Sophie tossed some photos on the table. 'Here are the photos of Rosie Dunn, now Elise Cadogan. But you see I needed you to think that, and I wanted to know where you stood. I wanted to be quite sure where you stood in regard to the murderess who is your daughter.'

'I need a strong drink,' said Ruth Dunn. She walked to the drinks tray, unstoppered the whisky decanter and poured a triple Johnny Walker Black.

'I was also sure, then, that I was not dangerous to the main game, the drugs game. In fact, perhaps amusing. So, I was played with. At *any* time might be disposed of. Perhaps it was the factor of a blood relationship? My cousin, Rosie Dunn, having consideration for her cousin, Sophie Parnell?'

'I doubt it.' Ruth drank deep and stared at the mahogany table the silver drinks tray stood on. The drawing room was done out in pale oyster. That was new by the looks of things, as were the chairs. As if Ruth Dunn had been comforting herself with interior decoration.

Outside was the large garden in its late season, where in spring rhododendrons would bloom and in summer wisteria in all its blue splendour would cascade over the stone walls. There in the pool, the carp would flick their tails while the kookaburras up there on the gum would dive and take them.

Sophie glanced down at her large Peruvian shopping bag. The tape would be turning, and Charlie Dunn was paying a lot of money for the truth.

'I think,' suggested Sophie, 'you had better begin at the beginning.'

Ruth Dunn looked away from Sophie and shivered. 'I think I would have killed you, somehow, if I had thought you would get this far. I would have found a way – to protect my family.'

'Start at the beginning, Ruth.'

'There isn't any beginning.' Ruth took another deep pull on her Johnny Walker. 'Can I have a cigarette, please? I've not smoked since I met Charlie. He didn't like a woman smoking, so I stopped.'

Sophie handed over her packet of Benson and Hedges.

Ruth, like the fifties girl she was, lit up with dainty gestures. She drew back, coughed and grew distant as the smoke filtered through her and drew her away into memories, into the past where she thought it must have started.

'You see, there was something the matter with her. I knew it when she was about seven or eight. She was good, too good. As if she missed out on a vital connection. She did what was expected of her. She was a sunshine girl, a nice girl they said. So I forgot, since that was what was said of Rosie. But then I would remember. It was as if she had a hole in her heart, a kind of psychic hole and love and affection just flowed through her.'

Ruth Dunn shrugged, her face again showed its fear. She looked at the garden. 'I'm going to take down that gum soon. It's taking too much goodness out of the soil and I don't like it. I'll plant a giant magnolia.'

Sophie felt herself sobering. Ruth did that to you. Ruth somehow dissolved horror and told you it didn't really exist.

'She was all right growing up. Charlie adored her, as our last born. She was OK at university. It all started when she went to Thailand, that evil bloody place. She turned into

111

one of them, accepting vice and corruption as part of life, of drugs and karma and destiny. She started to believe then in destiny. I *remember* that. She talked about people as just being masks, never real.

'Then she found people, *that man*, Rufus Stone. He thought she was OK. You know, she told me, about Janet, when, when she made me meet her. She talked about it coolly. She had watched Janet like *they* watched. Impassive, impersonal, like all those bloody orientals watch a sick cow, a dying child, a starving woman and then they think how they can make money out of them. Indifferent she was then. "Karma" *they* call it.'

Sophie was surprised, as no doubt the Buddha would have been by this interpretation of Buddhism. It was a fifties nightmare. Ruth had lived back there in the yellow peril days and then she'd got married.

'Why did Rosie Dunn decide to die?'

Ruth shook her head. 'Nothing can be said.'

'Then I'll ask Charlie Dunn.'

Ruth finished her whisky and stared at the gumtree. 'Charlie must never know.' She twisted her hands about trying to find a shape in them that would finish for good, with one squeeze, her nightmare. 'Rose is a wicked girl. A wicked person. Charlie must believe she died. That way she stays precious. That way my other kids don't know about her taint.'

'Why did she die?'

'I made her,' said Ruth Dunn slowly. 'I made her die. I told her that was what she must do. Die. For what she'd done. I believed she died and that she'd saved herself by dying.'

'And then?'

'You know. You know. The night of the inquest. The night Charlie met you. She rang. She said she had died but had decided on an early resurrection.

'She taunted me about Rufus Stone. She made me meet her. Down at Camp Cove. On the sand. She said, "Hello Mrs Dunn. My name's Elise Cadogan." She even had a faint American accent. Then I told her what Charlie was planning

112

and she said if I wanted Rosie Dunn to stay dead, I would tell her *everything* of your investigation.'

'And she came to her own funeral.'

'Yes, she came to her funeral. She told me the ashes were to be scattered at Camp Cove. She wanted to watch the ceremony and Charlie Dunn.

'Her brother and sister. Jesus,' Ruth shuddered, 'saying those loving things, those loving things for a dead sister.'

'And that's all?'

Ruth shrugged. 'You'll never know why. She promised me that. That she would never say.'

Ruth gazed out to the garden. 'There must be a technical term for what Rosie Dunn and Rufus Stone are. There must be some psychiatric description for it.'

Sophie stood up. 'And a moral description. Whole treatises have been written around people like Rosie Dunn. It all has to do with evil, Ruth. You are not wrong.'

They walked through to the front door, Sophie's brain clearing. She walked down the brick tiled path to the white high gate. Behind her Ruth Dunn shut the white front door cutting off the bricked-in foreyard along with the cat in its autumn coat.

Cliff was waiting in the car.

'Where to now, Sophie?'

'Downtown.'

'You OK?'

'No.' Sophie stared at the Victorian houses, the lace work and the vines baring now for a coming winter.

They drove downtown and parked under the Hilton. For diversion Sophie looked at a youngish woman who should have known better in her Alfetta GTV.

'Nice colour, that car,' said Cliffie to make conversation. 'Beige I suppose.'

'Ivory is what a lady like that would call it,' considered Sophie. 'Ivory has class. Beige is the colour of the carpet the lady will be rolling about on upstairs. Beige carpets, Cliffie. Ivory GTV Alfetta.'

Sophie got out and concentrated on the Bruce Springsteen

record the lovers were loving to. The man of course was dark and handsome, which showed the lady was probably suffering a lapse in taste.

Her face was familiar, but Sophie couldn't think where they'd met. Probably one of those raffish literary luncheons.

The statements for the public notary, a flash solicitor, took one hour for her and twenty minutes for Cliff. The tapes were sealed into hessian bags.

The statements were checked, signed, witnessed and sealed.

'Worth their weight in gold,' said the public notary, an old mate.

'Or heroin.' Sophie picked up her shopping bag. 'In fact much more. My life. Cliffie's life.'

'The instructions are quite simple. Should I or Cliffie vanish, they are to be released to the names I've left with you. Copies to the Press.'

The public notary, who had done his own typing, nodded and placed the statements into a wall safe. 'I'll have them in the bank tomorrow.'

◆ ◆ ◆

Out on the street, Cliff turned up the collar of his bum freezer jacket. It was a Bodie look-alike from the TV show 'The Professionals', and Cliff fancied the image.

'What now, Soph?'

'We consign the copies into the post. Double insurance.' She glanced up at the grey sky and the nearby skyscraper that housed the Rufus Stone enterprises.

Cliff licked the stamps on the three bulky packages. Sophie dropped them into the box.

'Let's go to a flick, Soph. I really liked that Mozart movie but I daresay it's too early to look again, what with the associations.'

'What about *The Killing Fields*?'

'OK. I'll shout you, Soph.'

'OK.' Soph took Cliff's arm and fell into her role of lady friend.

'What do we do afterwards?'

'We stay up, Cliff. We have to pay a visit and you have to be in top form. Top nasty form.'

'Who?'

'Janet Craig. You see, she knows why Rosie Dunn had to die.'

'I'll buy you an ice-cream, caramel flavour, at the flicks.' Cliff bussed Sophie.

❖ ❖ ❖

The alarm was set for two. Cliff rested easy like a child in the easy chair. Sophie put her feet up and watched the fire. Her hangover was passing with some aspirin and a large bottle of mineral water.

She didn't sleep but focused herself in on Ruth Dunn.

She'd gone there straight from the airport. She'd left Happy Hour bungalows with Cliff the day after Mary's body had been discovered. Washed in, to the chagrin of Kata bungalows, on their strip of beach. The French couple had left, too. Some instinct had kept them together until the airport at Bangkok. Then, with smiles and promises of writing they'd parted company, never mentioning again the occasion for flight.

The hours ticked, *Lente lente equi noctis*? Marlowe anyway, approximately. Couldn't remember her Latin anymore, or Marlowe. All those scholarly books she'd delved into, written from, thought about. All that solid research. Should make a book out of it. People did that all the time with their doctoral theses . . .

She glanced at the clock and realised she had slept. The alarm would go off and she would coax Cliffie into his role of heavy. Persuade him, needle him, get him mad.

She dozed again and dreamed of Janet Craig, sweet as pie sitting up in bed and talking about Rosie Dunn and what a saint she was – in the new dispensation.

❖ ❖ ❖

Cliffie concentrated on his driving and working up a good hate.

He had dressed the part: lean jeans bulging at the crotch, black t-shirt, leather jacket with silver studs on it. Sophie had slicked his hair back with some Brylcreem she'd dug out of the medicine cupboard.

Sophie kissed Cliff tenderly on the cheek.

Like getting into a difficult stage role, Clifford ignored her. He'd learned it at school, so Mrs Cray had told her, soon after she and Cliff had got together and Sophie had been taken home for the first of many Sunday night baked dinners.

Mrs Cray had watched him practising on his pillow after he'd been beaten up a few times at school. 'Had a natural talent,' Mrs Cray opined, 'just mixed up with his gentleness.' Mrs Cray had lit up a Capstan Plain and poured both ladies another glass of sweet sherry. 'Then he went out and beat up the kids that had beaten him up. Got messed up something dreadful. Wondered at the time if he'd affected his brain, but Mr Cray said that was unlikely. Kinda like going to war these days, Miss Parnell (it was still formal). And those bloody Marist brothers don't have any discipline from what I hear. What some of those kids need is a good hiding with the belt, same as we got.'

Cliff turned off Oxford Street, screeching the tyres, accelerating on the decline and whipping through the green lights one after the other. Ahead was Victoria Street.

They approached from Macleay Street, turning at the Wayside Chapel with its doctrinally dotty Minister and his large heart.

Cliff parked the car in the adjoining square.

Jamey was waiting in the shadows, dressed in old jeans and a scruffy blue jersey.

'How's it going mate?' Sophie gave Jamey a squeeze.

'Good, Sophie. He's left already. Just a quicky. Front door's open.'

'Great.'

'They've put forward my trial.' Jamey flashed a frightened smile. 'It's in a couple of weeks.' Jamey shuffled. 'One of

116

the shrinks reckoned I was psychopathic. I mean, I don't think so, do you, Soph?'

'Na, mate. Probably his own hang-up.'

'Another said I was disturbed. But he understood the compulsion.'

'Fair enough.' Sophie prodded Cliff forward before he went off the boil.

'Go home, Jamey,' she called over her shoulder. 'Nothing more to do now.'

'OK Soph,' Jamey loped off in the direction of his bedsit.

'How we gunna get in. I didn't bring my pick,' growled Cliff.

Sophie took a key from her bag. 'I went to see Janet's gentleman with the distinguished grey hair, Cliff, a friend of Daddy's. Met him at dinner once. I showed him the photo Jamey had taken and said I was doing a journalistic piece. He handed it over right smart.'

'He'll be getting his rocks off somewhere else now,' grunted Cliffie.

They walked up the stairs, Cliff leading light and sure like a cat.

Without fumbling, the key went straight into the lock. No need to tell Cliffie boy how to be, or to remember Jose-Maria or Jim Stokes, whom he'd never met.

The door opened, Cliff shone his pin-light, trod carefully then fast across the open ground to the half-open bedroom door.

Inside was a large double bed under a mirror in the ceiling.

Janet Craig was sleeping naked, her hand stretched out over her black silk sheets. There was a phallic-shaped candle burning on the dresser. On the floor surrounded by cream and tissues a magazine lay open at the bisexual endeavours of several ladies and several gentlemen. Music was turning on a tape. Low and soothing, post-coital music.

Cliffie switched off his pin-point and crept forward to the edge of the bed, face pasty-white and furious. Must do something to his blood supply, flooding the primeval brain section, thought Sophie.

Sophie turned on her battery torch and as good as any prison floodlight it caught on to Janet Craig. Cliffie grabbed the sleeping form, tossed it about and slapped it hard across the buttocks.

Janet Craig opened her mouth to scream but Cliffie's hand was across it.

'Well, well,' said Sophie in the background. 'That is just a small introduction to interrogation techniques in most South American prisons.'

'Ow, putta sock in it,' mumbled Cliff through clenched teeth, breath still coming hard and fast – a not unknown rhythm in this bedroom.

'The light, Clifford.'

Clifford leapt at the light cord and pulled hard. It came on in a pink blush through a large silk lampshade.

Sophie viewed the damage. Cliffie didn't like hitting ladies and the blows had been more sound than fury. Apart from a few welts loosing their colour, Janet Craig would be fit for business tomorrow. Could explain it away coyly as a customer hard to please. Madame Lash of Victoria Street taking some of her own medicine for a high fee.

'Let's start at the beginning,' suggested Sophie.

Janet remained silent.

'Ruth Dunn rang you and you and Rosie decided on strategy?' Sophie decided to start with a lie.

'No,' said Janet contemptuously. 'Rosie organised everything after she let Ruth know she was still alive. Ruth Dunn couldn't face *anything* that you couldn't report in the social columns! She only took orders, made sure what you knew we knew. She did it, too. She's a gutless bitch.'

'Did Rosie play the game with Sophia Mavrakis?'

Janet shrugged. 'Maybe.'

'What were you planning for me?'

'It depended. It depended whether we could work you into a suitable pattern. But we decided you were not dangerous enough but too dangerous to dispose of.'

Sophie glanced down at her large Peruvian shopping bag.

'And Jim Stokes? Who did in Jim Stokes? Did you know that was going to happen?'

'Get fucked.' Janet started to shake.

'And Sophia Mavrakis. Was she meant to die?'

Janet shrugged.

'Who broke into my apartment?'

'Rosie and Rufus, like you said. They felt like doing something crazy. They wore nylon gloves. No fingerprints.'

'Why?'

'To lead you on, to get you working on Jim Stokes.'

'Who killed him?'

Janet started shaking. 'There's nothing you can do against an empire. Rufus is back in town. Rosie's safe.'

'I know,' said Sophie. 'I saw his face in the evening newspapers. Opening a retarded children's home with the Prime Minister in tow.'

'He does a lot of good in his spare time.' Janet reached for her cigarettes and lit up with a gold Cartier lighter. 'You're outclassed, outgunned. Maybe Rosie went soft, since you're a cousin. Maybe Rufus decided your death wasn't worth it.'

'Didn't want two in the family?' asked Sophie.

Janet drew back, calm now. 'Well, that's a story too!'

'They're your gods, aren't they?'

'They supply,' said Janet. 'High-grade stuff, as a gift. They keep me going and when I want to, they'll pay for my treatment, but just now I don't want to cut the habit.' She stubbed out the cigarette in an ashtray. 'By the way, Rufus wants to see you. He thought you might pay a visit. I didn't. I didn't think you'd have the nerve.'

'Why did Rosie Dunn decide to die?'

'What did Ruth Dunn tell you?'

'She said Rosie died because Rosie was rotten with one spark of good in her and that spark Ruth blew on until it flamed and Rosie died.'

'Ruth hated Rosie from the start,' said Janet Craig. 'She never wanted her, so she told Rosie, right at the end. Rosie knows all that. But Rosie found a way of paying back that will eat into Ruth Dunn for the rest of her days.'

'What?' asked Sophie.

Janet Craig lay back on her bed and giggled.

'I think I'll go, Janet.'

'Please leave the key,' said Janet. 'The ageing knight rang and told me you'd been around. I told him not to worry. All old men get a bit weak in the loins and the head.'

Sophie took it from Cliff and placed it on the dressing table beside the pink phallic candle.

'Blow out the candle too,' Janet pulled up her black silk sheet. 'I forgot about it after the last customer left.'

◆ ◆ ◆

Sophie put the key into her own front door. No one was standing waiting with a sawn-off shotgun. Although then, she might have welcomed it.

Cliff brought Sophie hot milk in bed laced with brandy and sweetened with honey.

Sophie leaned back against the pillows. 'I feel kind of washed out, Cliff.'

'Me too,' said Cliff suffering his Catholic-conditioned conscience. 'Maybe I should send her some flowers tomorrow.'

'That's what you did for your mother. She told me, Cliff. After you'd had a barney as a little boy, you'd go out into the garden and pick dandelions and daisies and a few pansies and put a rubber band around them and deliver them at the front door.'

'Yeah, well . . .'

'Janet Craig's a nasty bitch, Cliff. It wasn't the drugs that did it. She was just waiting, like Rosie Dunn, for the right knight errant.'

'Why do you like me, Soph?'

Sophie put down the milk half-finished. 'Because you're sensitive and I've always liked sensitive men. And you're good, and I like good men too. And you write poetry that isn't half bad. You might even have genius bubbling away in there.'

'Like all the bloody Irish,' decided Cliff. 'Off the air, like bloody Yeats.'

'You've been reading him?'

'Yer, after that night the house was trashed. Bought the collected works. I keep them out in the loo.'

'Never noticed.' Sophie felt herself cheering up and decided against mentioning a perusal of her library would have provided a copy for nothing.

'I'm kind of sorry for Rosie Dunn, Janet and the rest of them.' Cliffie snuggled up. 'It's a real soap opera. Like they never find anything simple that matters. Just money and power. Like bloody Dallas. What a load of pricks!'

'*Vien dopo tanta erision, la morte e poi, e poi*? or something like that,' said Sophie.

'Verdi's *Othello*,' replied Cliff, snuggling more. 'You've said that before.'

16

The call came while Sophie, in her mother's caste-off satin dressing gown, stared at the restored Brett Whiteley. That had come at eight in the morning, delivered by Cliff's Central European mate, one of the Bondi Russians with a taste for mitteleurope forgeries that were doing quite well on the market.

It was a good repair job and her Celtic self was brooding over the sign and deciphering several contradictory meanings. Cliff was in the shower singing along with Bruce Springsteen. She glanced down at her thesis resting on her lap. Marlowe was important today. One bulwark for her and her spirit against the tides that lapped around.

She knew who would be phoning, just as she had known, at the beginning, she would know eventually what had happened to Rosie Dunn.

She picked up the phone.

'Dr Parnell?'

He did his research well. No one had called her 'Doctor' in a long time. He was also indicating the approach that would be made, or more its mode. It would be, she guessed, a conference.

'Speaking,' replied Sophie, mellowing into a long rusticated propriety.

'This is Mr Rufus Stone's private secretary. He would like to arrange lunch today at the Haute Couture, around one, if it is convenient – Mr Stone suggests that he might send a car for you.'

'Fine.' Sophie modestly drew the red satin of the dressing gown across her exposed stomach and took her feet off the fender.

'The car will pick you up around quarter to one?' The voice of the private secretary rose on the question and hushed into silence, as if contemplating its precarious eminence as private secretary.

Sophie launched into an over-ripe acceptance and hung up to Cliff's background applause. Then felt a little silly and went to pour the coffee made in her special Italian percolator, with coffee ground the only way it should be, to sand in Leichhardt, where half of Sicily was fomenting riot and disorder and consulting the *strega*, Sophia Mavrakis. Who had hung up when Sophie attempted another consultation.

Cliff sat down in his chair, a macho job in fading black-green leather, and dried his hair while Sophie poured the coffee, decanted the milk and laid out the croissants, butter and jam.

'That was Rufus Stone's secretary.' Sophie surveyed Cliffie who last night had been as tender as the night. Not to mention 'Shall I compare thee to a summer's day', before, during and *after*.

Sophie banished the faces of Mary and Sophia Mavrakis. Two blunderers playing with fire who hadn't thought their destiny would catch up with them. But the thing that bothered her was Jim Stokes. The body in the pool. Something was wrong there. She replayed Janet Craig on her bed, vagrant in her nudity, unconcerned as any porn queen under the studio lights. Until Jim Stokes had been mentioned.

'The information that Jim Stokes was going to give me didn't matter to Rufus Stone, why should it? He had put it there. Who then did it matter to, and why?'

'You mean you don't really see why he died?'

Sophie ignored the question. 'What reason would Rufus Stone have to kill him? He didn't need or want him dead, only discredited.'

'What was in the file Janet Craig gave you?'

'Telephone numbers, addresses and other numbers.' Sophie clicked her fingers. 'Bank numbers. Numbers of accounts.'

'Well?' asked Cliffie.

'I think,' said Sophie slowly, 'I was meant to do more or less what I did. I think those papers, so kindly handed on to me, were meant to end up where they did – in an export firm's office in Canberra.'

'Why?'

'I think Rufus Stone had managed to bring in Jim Stokes. Into his operation. I think he decided it was time to be rid of him. I think I was a courier carrying a death sentence. It's the only thing that makes sense.'

'You mean, he was kinda executed, officially, so to speak.'

'Yes.' Sophie drank down her coffee. 'My being there was the excuse. To put me off the scent. I would think Rufus Stone did it. But, in fact, I think there's been a trade-off, Cliffie. Jim Stokes for Rosie Dunn. Sean Long knew about her.'

'Her being alive?'

'Must have. It fits.'

'The payoff was Jim Stokes. And Janet Craig was frightened. She knew, or guessed, what had happened. Perhaps Janet has begun wondering how safe she is, if the situation changes.'

'But how can you be sure?'

'The body was floating, Cliff. It had been in there longer than ten minutes. Maybe for an hour or two. Maybe there had been another appointment before mine. Not with Rufus Stone's henchmen but one of Sean Long's executioners.'

'Well, we can retrieve the papers from the station.'

'No Cliff, we can't. They're gone. The door to the locker was forced. I went down there before leaving for Thailand. To check. They'd gone and a new key had been fitted. I was asked if I wished to lodge a complaint or apply for compensation. I didn't, of course.'

'Well, take care.' Cliff buttered another croissant.

'We have.' Sophie got up. 'We have.' She wandered upstairs and ran the bath.

It was an old Victorian one – deep, long and wide. Probably the whole family had got into it on bath night, or maybe they'd done it in tandem. She poured in essence of lavender and a good old-fashioned smell steamed back at her, fresh as a country garden as the label said. She got in and wallowed down, let her hair float out behind her as she had as a kid when she'd played at being the 'Lady of the Lake'. She came up for air and submerged again and wallowed and washed and wallowed some more.

The gas heater stayed on and the overflow drained away with a gurgle. The heater was a potential bomb but the water supply was limitless. Sophie went back into more happy memories.

When she felt clean again inside she got out, dried herself, rinsed her hair and blow dried it, got into a warmer chenille dressing gown and wandered through to the bedroom and opened the wall-length wardrobe. For a command performance, you dressed well, she reflected. She looked along the racks at the sixty or so outfits collected over the years, the earliest ones now back in high fashion.

She picked out an expensive-looking number in charcoal-grey wool and rummaged through her shirts until finding an oyster-coloured silk effort. One small hole under the armpit but that wouldn't show. Shoes in grey, too. A gift to Norma from the Kanak basher Henri, now back in town and still not knowing Norma's shoe size, which was quite large, as ladies feet tended to be when they'd started out life as men.

She dressed and rummaged again in the bottom of the wardrobe. This time to locate the shoe box where she hid her jewellery. She found it under a pile of dirty linen, pulled it out and rummaged again. She selected an emerald ring, a gold neckchain and a small bracelet of seed pearls.

In the bathroom a touch of 'Opium'.

She returned to the bedroom and sat down at her dressing table, pulling forward the old ivory tray her Gran had left her.

She began massaging on the face foundation. Then she got to work on the eyes – a grey-blue liner, a touch of mascara, a touch of rouge for the cheeks, natural lipstick. Eyebrows tidied up and a little eyebrow pencil applied. All a bit like the big occasion. Almost like facing your own death. Vanessa Redgrave as Mary Queen of Scots, in the film of the same name, working hard at the effect so that when her head was shown off to the crowd in the Great Hall at Fotheringay Castle it would look its charming best. 'In my end is my beginning' she'd said and stripped down to her red underskirt. Red for the martyrs.

Cliffie, downstairs, called out his goodbyes. On his way to the guard job. Twelve o'clock shift.

Molly Meldrum came in purring, jumped on Sophie's lap and admired himself in the looking glass.

At twelve Sophie heated some coffee and lit up the first cigarette of the day. She smoked it half down, then let herself out of the house and wandered up Oxford Street to the Church of St Francis, entered, genuflected and suppressed a desire to snort at the plasterwork kitsch that passed for religious art. She stopped at a side chapel where the only presentable statue presided over a small marble altar – the Risen Christ. She lit a candle and stood thinking of David and where he might be now.

She returned home obscurely comforted. It was time to call on Rufus Stone. Time to tether herself to the tree and see what the tiger would do.

The front doorbell rang. All around the Dobermans bayed. Cliff had switched on the alarm. Sophie switched it off and opened the door.

The driver in chauffer's uniform looked anxious. 'What have you got in there, a bloody Alsatian?'

'Several feral poodles,' said Sophie austerely. 'A girl can't be too careful these days what with muggings and rape and murder.'

She got into the car.

'Bloody animals,' said the driver ambiguously, swinging out smoothly and accelerating to processional speed.

❖ ❖ ❖

The Haute Couture had opened a few months before off Bayswater Road, and outside a doorman waited to assist the rich to alight on the swept pavement.

'Mr Stone will send for me after lunch, Miss.' The driver touched his cap and drove off.

Sophie adjusted her stockings and smiled graciously at the doorman.

She entered and looked around. From the wine-red carpet underfoot to the dark fumed oak barstools discretion reigned. A very European discretion. No advertisements of credit cards, no piped music. Just a head waiter correctly dressed and with polished shoes. Italian by the cut and leather.

'Yes, Madam?'

'Mr Stone. I'm expected.' Sophie found herself steeling up inside.

'Please follow me, Madam.'

She followed.

He was seated at a corner table, by itself, looking out on to a patch of harbour water with one yacht at distant anchor.

He was wearing a dark suit and a silk tie in deep blue. His face was tanned, and the hands on the table were thick and strong. Of course, Sophie remembered again. He ran every morning at Bondi Beach, rode the waves, came home, worked, went to a gym, played squash and worked.

The lips opened up to smile.

Sophie smiled back.

'Nice to see you Dr Parnell.'

Sophie allowed the waiter to seat her and glanced into Rufus Stone's face. It told her nothing.

'I've ordered martinis, very dry. I hope that's to your satisfaction.'

Sophie took out a cigarette. Rufus Stone was at the ready with a platinum lighter. How much of a dossier on her did he have? Quite large she would guess. Telephone taps, discreet surveillance, inside information from police. What else?

'How did you enjoy Thailand?' asked Sophie innocently. 'It's a pleasant time of year, although a little hot before the monsoon.'

An eyebrow went up. 'I've just come back from a business trip to Malaysia, a steel deal. Unfortunately, I didn't have time to holiday.'

First point to him. Some other passport.

The drinks arrived. Sophie took a long sip and felt the dry gin hit the spot. 'I found Kata Beach very pleasant. I do like the house on the headland. Rather Somerset Maugham. You know, where a writer could dream about things. Work well too, I should think.'

'It is very beautiful,' agreed Rufus Stone.

'The beauty was a little spoilt for me by a murder. Fortunately, I was with friends all evening and we discovered the body together. Such impeccable witnesses to the evening. The French Ambassador's personal secretary and a cultural attaché with a sense of fair play. Anyone who chases butterflies has to be a good man.'

Rufus Stone laughed and the skin crinkled. For a moment, inside, she felt a second face watching her, the one Rosie Dunn knew.

'Touché,' said Rufus Stone.

'Would you like to order?' asked the waiter.

'The seafood is excellent,' said Rufus Stone.

Sophie nodded.

'We could start with oysters and, since it's a cold day, move on to Maine lobster flown in this morning. Then, perhaps a slice of Black Forest cake, then Viennese coffee and cognac. After all, there's no need for you to watch the calories, Dr Parnell.'

Sophie caught the light edge of contempt and looked Rufus Stone straight in the eye.

Rufus Stone glanced around the room.

'One of your investments?' asked Sophie.

He nodded.

'So, Mr Stone, why have you called this meeting?'

'To warn and advise,' said Rufus Stone. 'And now you will give me your handbag.' He checked it briefly.

'I was given a brief Mr Stone, by the father of a girl who seemed to have suicided. It seems she never did, that she is alive and well, and you know her.'

Rufus Stone glanced at his gold signet ring set with a small blood ruby.

'I suppose,' said Sophie, 'my duty to my client is to tell him what I know, his wife knows, and Janet Craig knows. What too, Sophia Mavrakis knows, and what a man now dead called Jose-Maria knew. And I expect Jim Stokes knew.'

'Of the deaths Miss Parnell, which one do you personally regret?'

The oysters arrived with a bottle of chardonnay. Rufus Stone waved away the wine waiter, sipped, looked pleased and poured for them both.

'Neither,' said Sophie.

'That also is my feeling,' said Rufus Stone.

'However in both the deaths I am an accessory, to an extent,' said Sophie.

'But you didn't go to the police, Miss Parnell. Why not?'

It was the correct question. The question that would be asked in court.

Sophie took out a photograph and placed it on the table. Rufus Stone glanced at himself in the doorway of the Somerset Maugham house with Rosie Dunn.

'What guarantees of time and place? It could be anywhere.'

'A sworn statement.'

Rufus Stone gently shook his head. 'Even if Miss Rosie Dunn has come back to life, that would not put her in prison.'

'Sophia Mavrakis?'

Rufus Stone wolfed down the last of the oysters. Sophie finished hers and pushed away the plate.

'Why did you steal my licence?'

'For amusement, Sophie Parnell. A warning, too. Just as the knock-out in one was a warning.'

Again the second face and again public Rufus Stone.

'As I was saying. You were warned.'

'And Stokes?' asked Sophie.

But Rufus Stone changed the conversation to films while the waiter brought the lobster, shelled, soaked in garlic butter and lemon.

Sophie picked at the steaming white flesh and the fresh asparagus and the small, white new potatoes.

'What about Jim Stokes?'

'Stokes?' asked Rufus Stone, who ate methodically and slowly. 'Stokes was at first a spy. I don't like spies, Dr Parnell. None of us do. They can never really be trusted.'

'So you exposed his double game and traded him for silence on Rosie Dunn?'

Rufus Stone smiled.

'I have taken my precautions,' mentioned Sophie.

Rufus Stone nodded. 'All those tapes, mentioned over the phone, a visit to a public notary, copies posted where I don't know. Yes, Dr Parnell, you've taken precautions. But nothing could be proved, since no evidence you have would hold up in court. And since that is so, we reach an agreement as Rosie and I wish.

'You see, the most you could create would be a scandal. But then, I in turn, have the means to counteract that, to drag you in, show you up as a woman with parents who have taken money from me. And, perhaps on other matters, too.'

Sophie felt the lobster turning into a lump in her stomach. She concentrated hard, sipped some wine and it dissolved again and the acids went to work quietly and gently.

'I am not my father, Mr Stone.'

Rufus Stone gave her a soft glance. 'But really, it isn't a question of getting me. I cannot be got, Dr Parnell. At the most I can be smeared. But I too can smear back. And then there is the question of your client, Charlie Dunn, the innocent bystander. Of the Dunn family who would be destroyed? Your brief is to discover what happened to Rosie. It's quite simple. You now discover why Rosie Dunn died.'

'I wish to speak with Rosie Dunn.' Sophie steadied her glass.

Rufus Stone nodded. 'I know. It is the only logical ending. Now we are both at checkmate.'

'Stalemate, you mean.' She lit another cigarette.

'You shouldn't smoke so much, you're simply wide open

for a coronary or worse. Emphysema, lung cancer, but probably with your size, a coronary.'

Sophie accepted the advice, simply an appraisal this time.

'I have a ticket for you,' said Rufus Stone. 'You go again to Thailand. Alone this time. There's a plane leaving at five. Singapore Air. You are booked on it first class. The ticket was ordered by me. I have paid with a personal cheque both ways. It's your protection, if you like.'

Sophie declined the cake, but poured herself a coffee and added cream and sugar.

'Rosie will be waiting for you at the Somerset Maugham house, as you call it.'

He handed over a piece of paper. 'This is the travel agency I booked through.'

Sophie finished the coffee.

'It will be a surprising ending, the Rosie Dunn story.'

Rufus Stone stood up. 'I don't suppose we will bump into each other, socially. And, believe it or not, I was sorry about your brother David, but even that is not as it seems.'

'Do you love Rosie Dunn?' asked Sophie, ignoring her anger.

Rufus Stone looked at the white starched tablecloth, impeccable on his side, spotted with sauce on Sophie's, and declined to comment.

✦ 17 ✦

The plane took off on time. It left the ground and Sophie sweated. It found cruising altitude and speed. Sophie relaxed. Ten hours of suspended nothing.

Sophie reluctantly declined the first class supper, asked for water and took a Berocca. Smoked a cigarette, watched the movie, *Lace*. Went to sleep.

They arrived in the early light of dawn.

She put on her dark glasses, deplaned and went through customs.

She called a porter and walked behind him to internal flights. She checked in and sat in the air-conditioned anteroom. She read some Jane Austen and wondered if Cliff had remembered to get Molly Meldrum fresh liver.

She boarded.

An hour and half later the plane touched down at Phuket airport.

She took a taxi.

The rice paddies were starting to green since the first showers were beginning to fall heavily, as they did, like leaden drops. The jungle stretched ahead and the hills. Then the distant view of the sea, the stretch of bay and Kata Beach in its half moon, the descent along the dust road past the school in its flat paddock where the kids played their drums, the magisterial cane at rest on a chair.

Then the swoop around the corner.

Happy Hour bungalows were quiet.

Sophie got out.

Luk was waiting at the bar, a sarong wrapped around him, face sheened by sleep.

He took a key off the board. 'We give you same bungalow, Sophie. For good luck.' He smiled at his joke.

'I'm going to sleep, Luk.'

She unfold a mosquito net, showered and got herself into bed.

She woke up at two, showered again, put on her bathing suit and took a large beach towel someone had placed in her bathroom while she slept.

The restaurant area was almost deserted. Except for Allan, in his sarong, playing darts by himself.

'Hi Allan,' said Sophie. Allan paled, as if he had seen a ghost.

'Been away on a trip?' asked Allan, ignoring the police, Jose-Maria and the headlines.

'Yes.'

'Brothel in town burned down.' Allan scored a bull's-eye. 'They reckon about five or six died. Some woman in town's demanding an investigation. She says the girls were chained to the beds, like they do in India. You know, heroin addicts. They reckon, too, some of them were beaten to death and they're going to dig up the backyard. The Chief of Police might be transferred.'

'A change is as good as a holiday.'

'Yer.'

'Money come through yet, Allan?'

'I'm OK.' Allan threw a ten. 'I'm practising to play with Conan tonight.'

'What's the news of Mary's death?'

Allan's hand hardly shook. 'They reckon it had something to do with some woman. You know, he used to take whoever he felt like. Someone's brother did it they reckon.'

'Quite unusual,' said Sophie, 'that degree of passion. In a brother, I mean. Around here. Most of them seem only too anxious to sell them off.'

133

Allan managed a laugh. 'See you later.'

'Yeah.'

The house still stood, on the low-slung slice of headland. The roof was still painted a dull rust brown and the wood oiled. It was, Sophie thought, settling herself down in the sun, the sort of place you'd expect in Maine, or maybe Cape Cod, or somewhere down the coast from Sydney before they'd got posh and tasteless.

She didn't know why, but she had half-expected it altered, like a stage set. Acts I and II had passed; the opera was entering Act III. A tragedy, a new death? Her death?

She swam and lay again in the sun, then ordered a late lunch from the shack restaurant. It was better food than the Haute Couture. Better cooked, in the *wok*, with the embers glowing, and a tang of wood smoke in the noodles.

Boss dog was on the beach, amiable and large of head. She gave him the fish head. He snapped it down. So much for the myth of fish bones and dogs. Maybe only Australian dogs.

She finished, paid and wandered along to the end bar, perched on a flat rock. Dap, the owner, smiled vaguely at her and offered her a roach. Sophie, not much into weed, took a puff, helped herself to another small beer and turned to look at the paradise that Rosie Dunn must be looking at. She opened her camera, took a couple of photos of Dap, focused in on the beach and Allan talking to a man who looked Australian and photographed them, too.

'What will they do about the murder, Dap?'

Dap came out of his dream and took off his headphones. 'I dunno, man. Maybe they forget about it. He was only *farang*, you know, like you. Just come and go. Maybe he see too much, open mouth too wide. You know, man, karma. Can't avoid it, man.'

Dap turned on his ghetto blaster. 'Bruce Springsteen,' muttered Dap. 'Man how I adore you, like I adore Buddha.'

❖ ❖ ❖

Evening arrived and she walked up to Happy Hour bungalows. The pigs were rootling in bushes, the Chinese rooster with his hens came up from the road edge, feathery tail held high. Far in the distance an electrical storm was building. Some rain fell in large drops and stopped again.

Luk came out with his guitar. Toddling behind him was a small boy, and what must be the wife.

'You happy here?' The wife asked. Sophie ordered a gin and tonic.

Luk sat down with his guitar. 'I most happy. Nit returns from Bangkok. My mother say that until we have proper place for little boy he must stay with her. Nit go and tell her we have proper rooms and all is well. We haven't but we want our baby back. My mother, she keep him forever if she can. She live alone now in big house and she say "I have garden for him to play in". But this too is garden.'

Sophie took her drink and Luk tuned and started playing.

'I make up this song, Sophie, for when my beloveds come back and I sing it.' The music was a mixture of Jackson Five with some older sadder melody. Luk started to hum along and the inspiration struck again. *'here I am, my son and Lamb/I most happiest man in land,/All is good, all is round/My son is home, like flower in hand/So crap your hand, crap your hand.'*

That, apparently, was the chorus. None of them of course could get out an 'L' but sometimes the gods spoke in their own way.

Luk played it several times as little Luk danced around, almost in time, almost balanced. Behind him, Sophie could see the shadow of Mary: *Beat Me, Bite Me, Suck Me, Fuck Me* in large red letters on his t-shirt.

'What about Mary?' she asked.

'They bury him in Phuket,' said Luk. 'Mother no can come. Conan pay for funeral. Maybe also take money. Mary leave money around in house. Conan live there now with his woman. He keep on old woman who cook for Mary and wash and dust.'

Little Luk wobbled and sat down on his bottom. He started to cry. Big Luk, with a loving glance, put down his guitar and picked him up for a cuddle. And he tried out the verse and chorus again.

Allan came in, and since the love room was filled up and Allan couldn't persuade them that they should love him still, even though his money hadn't arrived, didn't smile and didn't laugh and didn't say, as he might have once, 'You've got it wrong, Luk. Clap, clap your hand, not shit on it.'

Sophie didn't feel she knew Luk at all, so she said nothing.

Then a jeep ground to a halt outside in a swirl of dust and clanging gears.

Conan the Barbarian with his flint eyes came up the steps, gave Sophie an appraising glance, broke into a feral smile.

'Say, you back, man. Great, man. Great. How long you stay this time?'

'As the mood takes me,' Sophie finished her drink.

Conan was still vibrating at ten times the rate of anyone else. Only the former heroin queen was in mourning: black shirt and trousers, white face and white smile and white teeth.

'We moving off soon,' Conan said. 'Maybe we go back to Goa. I've got some business I can do there. Buy up old musical instruments. Man you can make a fortune in bazaar there and at Bombay if you know what you look for. Friend of mine make fortune.'

❖ ❖ ❖

Sophie wandered down to Madame Tui's and ordered a drink.

Allan was there. He was sitting with a lady called Io. A Dutchman was sitting alone. 'He's a croupier,' said Allan, 'in Holland.'

'Me Nit,' said a bargirl to the the Dutchman. 'How you, big boy, you wanna take me dancing over at disco?'

Allan laughed and Madame Tui, behind the bar, watched. Somewhere in the backroom, her baby cried. One of the girls got up and went to see.

The fairy lights flickered as the current went down then came up strong again and again it was Christmas. Tui brought over Sophie's beer. Far on the horizon the lightning flickered.

'Not many tonight, Allan.' Allan giggled a bit. High, Sophie thought, and swallowing beer like there was no yesterday.

'All gone home. It gets bloody hot before the monsoon. Looks as if it might break.'

Allan looked out to the road. The jeep of the Chief of Police slowed down. The Chief of Police looked in. Allan smiled and waved. Madame Tui ran out with three bottles of beer. The girls smiled and waved as if he might, after all, be Father Christmas.

'He's a Big Man,' said Allan. 'Very Big Man. They say he'll be next governor of the province.'

❖ ❖ ❖

The summons came for eight o'clock the following evening.

Sophie was taking a walk along the beach. The air was like a crystal ball. The stars hanging in clarity. In the far distance, growing into the crystal ball, was the storm, heavier now and coming close. The lightning flashed across the clouds, played with itself, fused into colours and became a wind of light.

Looking back, in the near distance, the five shack restaurants and Dap's end bar became one large floating barge, lit in orange and blue, red and pink, gold and yellow. An amusement park, fronting deckchairs spaced evenly along on the sand before a flat sea. A Fellini set. *Il Nave Va: The Ship Goes Onwards*. Where?

Spaced nowhere was the house on the headland. Up there a light went on.

Sophie walked down to Dap's bar and the image broke and became, again, shacks, children and coloured lights strung from beam to wooden beam.

Dap offered Sophie a gin and tonic and a note. Sophie searched for her cigarettes while Dap watched.

'Storm is usual,' said Dap. 'Maybe rain, maybe not. Is like great electrical sea up there.'

Sophie wished she had taken a swim.

'Looks like one of those war movies.' Dap polished some glasses. 'Like when the commandos come ashore in rubber boats.' Obligingly the bank of cloud flickered from one side to the other in white light and lit up the beach and sea in grey. 'Then,' said Dap, enthusiastically, 'they come ashore and kill a Nazi sentry, then go into the jungle.'

'Some war!' Sophie opened the letter. It was a simple message from an empress to a rather irritating subject: 'I'll be pleased to talk with you now.' It was left unsigned. Rosie Dunn wasn't taking any written risks.

'I take you up,' said Dap smiling. 'You want another drink first?' Sophie handed over the glass. Dap served his usual liberal idea of hospitality and added lemon and the rest of the tonic.

Sophie just as suddenly wanted to get moving but Dap, sitting back on his six-foot long bar, was relaxing into the night, eyes bright like a cat's, with electricity.

'OK,' said Sophie, 'who gave you the note?'

Dap nodded up to the headland. 'A man. He gave it to me.'

'European?'

Dap shook his head. 'Thai man. From somewhere else. He watch you come along beach and he know you come here for drink. You always do.'

Truth or lies. It didn't matter. If they wanted to take her out they could do it at any place and any time.

'Let's go.'

'You no finish.'

Sophie shrugged.

Dap took the glass and finished it for her.

He whistled. A waiter came out to the end restaurant and wandered across the sand to mind the bar.

They walked through the restaurant the waiter had come from and out on to the dust road.

The storm was performing a panorama, moving closer, menacing in those jagged streaks that clashed and fought with each other and might at any moment give up on the game and take a look at the earth.

It was, Sophie decided, a little like Rosie Dunn's mind. Deep down, she suspected, was a clashing of forces, of electrical impulses that hit at each other then fused into intention. Or simply played with the idea the way the storm was. Perhaps, she thought, as the wind arrived, that had been the attraction between Rufus Stone and Rosie. Two elementals, two creatures of energy who knew only release and pleasure. One minor deity who had done well with the other who had come in on his slipstream.

They arrived at the large iron gate.

The gate was opened.

The guard was carrying a very nasty gun.

Sophie raised her arms, and behind her Dap giggled.

The guard shrugged.

No need for a search she thought a moment later. Whatever was concealed in the few possibilities of the female anatomy could hardly be pulled out in a bar-room shootout.

Somewhere behind her Dap had vanished, as had the guard.

She walked up the path to the door and knocked. A moment later, feet padded across the floor. The door opened.

'Hello,' said Rosie Dunn. 'Thanks for coming.'

She stood aside and Sophie entered the room. It was a large beach house of the old style—bare varnished boards, a fireplace at the end, comfortable chairs in rattan, large windows that framed the view as she knew they would.

Rosie Dunn stood near the chair where she had been sitting. Across from her was another chair, for Sophie Parnell.

'I remember seeing a picture of you when you were hockey captain at Chamfield,' said Rosie Dunn. 'I was in the third form then. I think we might have met later, at family gatherings, but I don't really remember.'

She was wearing a long yellow silk gown, cut simply and falling to her feet. Her features were more angular than Sophie recalled, with high cheekbones that time had exposed. She had topaz eyes and her blonde hair had been washed and combed straight down her back.

Rosie sat down and gestured to the chair. A servant materialised with a silver tray. He put it down, poured a gin and tonic for Sophie and a tonic with ice and lemon for Rosie Dunn.

'I thought you'd like your usual drink,' said Rosie. 'Who

139

drinks whisky in your house?' she asked a second later.

'I do, in winter. Cliff and I like a nightcap.'

'Like Charlie Dunn,' Rosie relaxed. 'He always liked a Johnny Walker Black before retiring.'

Sophie rested in silence. She was, after all, here by invitation, and Rosie Dunn, whatever had happened, was no longer part of a world Sophie knew. She looked like a boat gently rocking in mid-ocean. Sophie didn't much like the sensation she got from looking at her.

Rosie Dunn reached down to a pile of books beside her, played with a few titles as if looking for her own role, then sat up. For the first time she looked directly at Sophie, and the topaz eyes filmed over.

'Why did you do it?' asked Sophie. 'Why did you pretend to suicide or murder?'

Rosie laughed quietly. 'It was an open verdict.' She got up and walked across to the sofa, one of those low comfortable efforts you might find on the porch of a house at Palm Beach. She stretched out, role decided. 'At the beginning, I thought you should be put away. Or at least, seriously put off. You didn't know anything about me and we could stop you ever finding out.'

'Like Sophia Mavrakis?'

Rosie shrugged. 'Then I became kind of interested in it. It was like a game of chess. Calculating your moves, ringing Janet and Ruth Dunn, checking on Sophia Mavrakis through other contacts. It was like planning a war campaign. That's why, I suppose, we decided, once we had you checkmated, to let you in a little on our life. My life really. My new life.'

'I could still talk.'

Rosie laughed. 'No you couldn't, and you know that. You destroy Ruth Dunn, you destroy Charlie, even more Charlie, who's your employer, but we'll come to *that* later. Then there's your parents, and the money Rufus paid over and the allowance he's paid since. Then there are two, no three cheques paid into your bank account on Rufus Stone's signature.'

Sophie felt her hackles go up. 'What cheques?'

140

'Well, we decided to cloud from the beginning. If anything ever did come out, against Rufus I mean, how would you explain it? We would have an explanation, at least Rufus would. He has all the expertise, but you?'

'How much?'

'Thirty thousand dollars in three cheques. It was worth the expense.' Rosie sipped her drink. 'We knew you were hopeless about money, never looked at your statements. It was a gamble, but it worked.'

'I see.'

'Then there is Cliff. A smear, maybe a crime he never committed. Five years ago, we were told, he was suspected of a hold-up job in Marrickville. They never found the gang. Cliff could have been one. It's not difficult to re-open an investigation. Fresh evidence, someone grassing as they call it – for a small sum of course.'

Sophie felt herself cooling down in her stomach. It was a good sign.

'Then your mother. Did you know she had an affair? Believe it or not with her parish priest, twenty years ago. The Church cut your father in on some land deals so he wouldn't go ahead with the divorce and citing Father whatever. So you see, there are a lot of points of threat now, not to your life, but to your happiness, if you know what I mean.'

Sophie did.

'A lot has happened to me, Sophie, since I died. But I suppose I'd better talk rationally. You know, like an honours graduate in anthropology.' She glanced over at the wall where the scroll was framed. 'I told Ruth Dunn to hand it over. A posthumous degree.' Rosie giggled.

But that wasn't the point either. She knew it and Sophie knew it. Whatever the well-springs of Rosie Dunn's being, they were flowing silent and dark, and she enjoyed that.

Then Sophie had the feeling, as with Rufus Stone, of another face looking through Rosie's eyes, like a cat watching a mouse. She lost it again when Rosie Dunn decided to play the ingénue.

'It's all a bit mixed up for me. I guess in myself. You

141

know, my real self, not the shit you show your family and friends.'

Rosie was warming up to an old role, one she had played many times in her head. One she had always wanted an audience for.

'I always knew life wasn't like the headmistress said at school. I mean the reality was out the window, wasn't it? You know, the whores waiting around in the evenings for customers, the drugs, the hustle of things.

'I could never see the point of marrying some nice rich young lawyer. Of course, I had my crushes. I held a light for some of those nice Eastern suburbs boys, but they all finally bored me. They were so thick, so dense really. No panache. I preferred Darlinghurst and the whores. Things went on down there. People got done in, parties happened, someone was raped, someone got beaten up. It had more colour.

'So I couldn't see the point in closing your eyes and opening your legs.

'You know, Charlie Dunn used to give abortions. Ruth told me, before I died of course, quite a long time before I died. They'd had a fight and Ruth had no one else to turn to.' Rosie Dunn's lips curled. 'She got pissed and said it was only for society ladies who would later help *him*. He was in his last year at medical school. He never charged either.

'That was clever wasn't it? Charlie Dunn had his head screwed on the right way. It was also quite clever to marry Ruth. She was eight years older than he but she had a trust and quite a lot of liquid cash.'

Sophie felt somewhere a shiver starting. Like a sudden fever when the body was throwing off poison in its system.

'I see,' said Sophie, who did see.

'Well, we are really talking about Rosie Dunn and how she turned out the way she did. These days, by the way, I'm called Elise Cadogan.'

The storm was coming closer and the lights flickered on and off the bay.

Rosie got up and put on a cassette. It was familiar – Cleo Laine singing *Gymnopédies*.

'It's all I pinched from your house.' Rosie sat down again. 'I like John Dankworth and his flute. Cleo's great too. I took it because I'd heard it on the radio that day.'

Rosie got lost in her thoughts. 'They thought that I was a nice girl. Of course, Ruth always loathed me, but that was because Charlie liked me. But the rest always said, that nice Rosie Dunn, always behaves herself, always says the right thing. A prefect at school. An open girl they said. A good girl who could turn her hand to anything.'

That seemed to be Sophie's opening. 'And did you?' she asked, watching the body language as Rosie changed position and put a cushion protectively against her stomach.

'In a way. Yes, in a way. But that happened with Rufus. When we met. He, up here arranging high finance, all of two years ago or so. But strangely the real bonding took place a bit later. It concerns you, too. When you go through suffering something links you, as Rufus said. And we are linked.'

'I know,' said Sophie. She lit up a cigarette.

'But you didn't guess,' Rosie Dunn looked annoyed, 'how it happened. That's the real surprise.

'You see, we were in Canberra and I hadn't quite grown up enough, then. Rufus said that was the reason I had been silly. And Rufus wants you to know this – I was at his party with him. People thought I was just a casual lay. He had a lot of them, once, after he divorced his last wife. But I wasn't.

'Anyway, Rufus fell asleep. A bit pissed I guess. I got bored. I wanted to do something. I remember wandering around that large house. The Prime Minister had been there, Ambassadors, a few tame writers and kultur vultures. Then it was all over.

'I wanted to drive. So I went to the car; the keys were in it.

'I loved that feeling in the Jag.' Rosie's eyes grew dreamy. 'Rushing through the night. You can have wonderful fantasies when you've got the foot pressed down.

'I must have been having a fantasy when I saw this figure in front of me. I didn't see who it was then. But you know, don't you?'

Sophie nodded.

'It was awful seeing his body catapault up into the air and smash against the windscreen. I don't know how he didn't manage to break it.

'There was blood everywhere and there he was, smashed up. I stopped. The police came. Then I spoke to Rufus on the car telephone and he came and we left.

'I had nightmares for weeks. But I knew I didn't need to go to a shrink. It was really a growing-up experience. And it wouldn't have helped Rufus to have his name in the papers, and besides they would have taken away my licence and that wouldn't have helped anyone, and I might have gone to prison. And think what that would have done to Charlie Dunn! His favourite daughter in prison!'

'Do Charlie and Ruth both know?'

Rosie ignored this.

'I dreamed about his blood,' she went on in a little girl's voice. 'It was really horrible for me. But then Rufus took care of it all and the nightmares stopped.

'I think when things like that happen you kind of fuse inside with the other person. It's a bit like Vietnam. You know, buddies who really care for each other. So we became more than lovers. More than husband and wife.

'I knew, then, about Rufus' business. I knew he had to move into drugs. If he didn't, someone else respectable would. In fact, a few have. But Rufus is Numero Uno. So he started to really explain things to me and I did some missions for him.'

Rosie sipped on her tonic. 'You see, Rufus really rules the state. He rules the politicians, the judges, the media. He rules everything. And when you are Numero Uno, you have to rule drugs. Rufus hates heroin, but then he didn't create it.'

'I wonder who did,' said Sophie, barely managing to keep her voice level.

'God, I suppose,' decided Rosie Dunn.

'I left home then. I had my flat at the Cross. Charlie paid half and Rufus paid half. I never told Charlie that.

'Janet and I shared with Luk. He was only my boyfriend

for a while and Rufus didn't mind since he often had to be away. We never met there of course. We met down at Camp Cove, in the apartment there. That's when I chose the name Elise Cadogan. It was kind of aristocratic.'

Rosie sipped on her tonic, grimaced and went to the open window and threw it on to the lawn. At the drinks table she poured herself another one. 'I like the bubbles,' she confessed, 'and I like them cold.'

'What about Jim Stokes?'

'He wasn't reliable,' said Rosie Dunn. 'He was in narcotics, you know, but Rufus cut him in. First he threatened him, since Jim Stokes, who was a respectable married man, liked a boy now and then. Not down in Sydney but up here, where AIDS hasn't got yet.

'Rufus had the photos. But then Jim Stokes let drop to his other employers that I was still alive and that I meant a great deal to Rufus Stone, and they put pressure on Rufus and then you came on the scene.

'There were two possibilities. The first was what I favoured. Somehow to get you and Jim Stokes together in my flat and then have you both killed. That way the papers would be more valid. They would show Jim Stokes in drugs and a front man for the Thais and Chinese. That way we would checkmate his other employers who might have given evidence at a Royal Commission the government was thinking of setting up.

'And Rosie Dunn would stay dead. But Rufus said it was too dangerous and, besides, we had to think about David already dead and the friends you had.

'He was probably right in thinking you would be more dangerous to us out of the game. So instead, we just used you as a messenger to tell Jim Stokes' other employers what he had been up to. You know, double dealing.

'And then they dealt with Jim Stokes and the pressure came off Rufus with regards to me.

'I'd been stupid once myself, but not like Jim Stokes. Luk really was responsible but I guess he didn't know who Rufus Stone really was. He used me to do some dealing and some of Rufus' enemies used that to try and get at

145

him. Rufus found out and gave me such a hiding.'

The boredom Sophie was beginning to feel vanished.

'So I went home, that night, to Charlie Dunn.'

Rosie spoke about him as another man and she looked at Sophie curiously, as if trying to evaluate how she would react.

Sophie felt herself prickling again with nerves.

Then Rosie changed tracks.

'You see, the reason Sophia Mavrakis was punished was because she had been well paid for a service. She had a lot of Italian friends, a lot of people in small-time crime, and we needed a body when it was time for me to vanish for good. Sophia Mavrakis found the contact. And she guessed about the other thing. At the time Rufus and I both thought we should kill her, then we decided we would just punish her.'

'Did you do it?'

Rosie shook her head. 'Rufus did. I watched. I don't think she knew it was me or him. She didn't have that much time anyway to think about it.'

Sophie knew, like a good actress, Rosie was delaying the revelation, playing with the atmosphere.

'So I went home to Charlie Dunn,' said Rosie Dunn again. 'Rufus had been a beast and Charlie put a couple of stitches in my lip.' Her voice grew dreamy again.

'I told Charlie other things too, and we drank some whisky and then we got drunk and went to bed. We slept in my room. Mum was away for the weekend up at Palm Beach.

'Charlie said it was the greatest thing that had ever happened. I had to help him, of course, to make it happen. He would never have dared if I hadn't helped him to see what he wanted.'

'Does Ruth Dunn know?'

In sync, somewhere off-stage, a baby began crying. 'He's a little boy, Charlie's and my son.' Rosie stood up. 'I had him in a private clinic in Bangkok. There was a doctor there with me, for quite a time, and a trained nurse. I didn't breast-feed him, the milk just wouldn't come enough. I was worried too, about disease. You know, Asia and the rest. But he's really flourishing.'

She took Sophie's arm. 'Come and see.'

They walked through the hall into a nursery. The basinette was covered in mosquito netting. Beside it was a chair with a young Thai girl in a nurse's uniform sitting in it. She looked up and smiled.

'That's Rufus.' Rosie Dunn lifted the net.

Baby Rufus, son of Charlie Dunn, lay sleeping with the same fair hair as Rosie and Charlie Dunn and the same line of jaw.

'What did Ruth say?'

'Ruth has always hated me,' noted Rosie, unemotionally, 'from the start. Maybe because she decided her marriage was a mistake. Maybe because Charlie loved me but had only used her. She told me she knew I was abnormal. Mad, she called it. She said it must be some strain from the Dunns since none of her family had ever had a monster like me in it. She said she would never tell Charlie Dunn. Then she went to town on me. She said I should die. She said that something as rotten as me shouldn't live.'

'She knew about the drugs and Rufus.'

'Oh yes,' said Rosie, her face lighting up as she took the curled fist of the baby's in her hand. 'Oh yes, I told her everything. I probably made it worse than it was. I also told her about David, and Luk. And Janet. Janet and me, I mean. But that was just playtime really. Just an experience.

'Ruth went right off the air. I started crying. I suppose because I knew she'd never loved me. Not that I loved her either. I've only ever loved Rufus.'

'Why did you disappear?'

'Because Ruth wanted me to. Ruth wanted me dead, the baby dead, all of me dead. So I agreed. I arranged it with Sophia Mavrakis. She was paid well for the body she located.'

'But you wanted Ruth to suffer?'

'Yes.' Rosie smiled. 'She never had been my mother and I wanted her to suffer. I taunted her. I knew she would suffer. Guilt. Jealousy over me and Charlie. Scared too, for the other kids. My brother and sister.'

'And then on the day of the inquest, when Charlie Dunn

147

met you down at the *Queen Elizabeth*, I rang her up and said "Hello Ruth, this is your former daughter speaking". She almost died from shock.'

'And you've been playing her ever since?'

Rosie nodded. 'Let's go back to the sitting room.'

Sophie followed. The pieces of the jigsaw fitted tighter together.

'Rufus and I took the body up to the Gap. We did it late in the night. It was easy, but dangerous, you know. That's the real fun we've had. Coming close but not slipping over.

'She was some girl that OD'd on heroin. There was a lot out on the street just then that was stronger than usual. I think chemically different or something like that. Anyway, we dressed her in my clothes and I put on her finger the ring Charlie had given me. It could have been me, too. She had no head left. That was part of the deal. You know, dental records.

'Rufus did a mock funeral service and we sang a hymn, sort of, then over she went. Fell like a sack of spuds then kind of flew and then she vanished.' Rosie's voice grew quiet. 'It was a strange sensation to see yourself, in a way, jumping off. But it was the end of the old life.

'We knew from the tides it would be weeks or months before they found me.'

'It was months,' said Sophie.

'Then I left my bag there, and my shoes.' Rosie clasped her hands together. 'The girl's body looked just like me, like a lot of Australian girls, really, only when they found me, it didn't matter. All bloat and corruption, I understand. Identified only by the ring.'

She glanced out into the garden. The storm would not break. It was content with its violet and red and purple play.

'Like a fireworks display over Sydney Harbour in Festival Week,' said Rosie Dunn. She glanced at her watch. 'It's almost time for you to leave.' She gave a small secret smile. 'But not for heaven.'

'What will you do?'

'Oh, Rufus takes care of everything. He has an apartment

148

in New York in the East Sixties. I went there last month to do it over. Wonderful penthouse with a view of the East River. We'll set up money for me there. A trust, I guess. Occasionally, too, I'll pop back to Sydney. Just to look around. But my real life will be there.'

'And your parents?' Sophie couldn't stop herself. It was the bog Irish blood loyalty. Whatever the blood. It was a stupid question and she regretted asking it, but Rosie Dunn took it in her stride.

'Maybe, one day, I'll see Charlie Dunn again. Maybe one day he'll get a big surprise and maybe not. Maybe when he gets his knighthood for services to the medical profession, I might go and see him with little Rufus. But not Ruth.' Her voice turned cold. 'Ruth can sweat out her life, never knowing. I told her when I met her down at Camp Cove that she might be *personally* surprised again one day.'

'Why did you destroy the painting?' This too was a silly question, but Rosie Dunn was eager enough to answer.

'Oh, I wanted you to think it was someone really spiteful. To make you angry so you'd go on. It was becoming such a game for Rufus and me. Not that we'll play another like it in a long time.'

'Is that it, the excitement of it, a game?'

Rosie nodded. 'No one,' she said, 'has an idea, except you. And you are tied.'

Sophie nodded. 'I know.'

'You can never tell,' said Rosie Dunn, 'since no one would believe you.'

Sophie glanced at the Khmer Buddha in a niche and at a beautiful bas-relief, in the shadow, of some dancing women.

Through the storm noise came the sound of a helicopter.

'This place is used, isn't it, for heroin importation into Oz?'

Rosie nodded, then took some binoculars from the mantelpiece. 'Come outside.' Sophie followed her on to the lawn and out towards the promentary.

Rosie handed her the glasses. 'Out there, you'll see a freighter. I think at the other end it's offloaded on to fishing boats. Up and down the coast from north of Darwin to around Noosa.'

Sophie took the binoculars and focused. It was a largish vessel with brown-stained sides and a newly painted funnel.

'Maybe I should hitch a ride?'

Rosie shook her head. Her hair began to winnow as the helicopter, now overhead, came into land.

Some garden lights came on, and striding through the gate was the Chief of Police and next Military Governor of the province.

'You see, important men are involved with Rufus. It's all very top drawer.'

Rosie walked forward. She started saying something else but the noise drowned out the rest and only her moving lips and smiling eyes indicated her happiness.

Three men jumped out of the helicopter as the motor cut. They walked into the house and returned, moments later, with three large cases. They loaded and returned for more.

'It's all purified up here. Not like the Mafia, who use Sicily or the South of France. Our way, there's little chance for the Oz police to catch on to the operation.'

The helicopter took off into the storm, arched out across the bay, vanished. 'It's landed,' said Rosie, 'on the deck.' She put the binoculars down on the garden table.

Ten minutes later the helicopter reappeared. 'Now,' said Rosie, 'it's time for you to leave me.' Luk appeared at the gate carrying her luggage.

'There might be a small surprise for you, Sophie,' said Rosie kissing her on the cheek. 'Something quite exciting in its own way.'

Sophie waited. The chopper landed. The next Military Governor, all smiles, hefted her case on board.

'You're booked,' said Rosie, 'on an early morning flight from Phuket and that night from Bangkok to Sydney.'

Rosie waited while Sophie climbed aboard and strapped herself in.

'Of course,' said the empress, cool and distant, 'you can't come back here. Not ever. To Thailand.'

'But I can live in Sydney?' asked Sophie, who wanted a few moments to prepare herself, if it was the worst.

'Oh yes, the surprise isn't flying without a parachute. There's no point. We've won the match, check from the white queen to every piece left on the board.' Rosie waved her hand and again the mischievous smile lit up her face. 'Give my love to Ruth. Tell her the baby's fine and I'm fine.'

The chopper rose. The pilot and co-pilot gave a thumbs up, hovered, then swept out across the bay. The storm burst ahead and below was Happy Hour bungalows.

They landed at Phuket airport.

Sophie took her case from the smiling off-duty airforce officers and walked through to the waiting room. She opened her suitcase. Her passport and tickets were on top. She glanced around, feeling her body now dissolving into a cleansing sweat.

She walked into the ladies with the suitcase. There was no point in waiting until a Bangkok hotel room. Systematically she went through the toilet bag and threw away the toothpaste, the talcum powder, the face cream. Then she began unpacking. She found what she was looking for, tucked into the middle of her sarong. It was a small plastic packet with white powder inside. She threw it into the pan and pressed the flush button.

She returned to the bag. Rosie Dunn's little joke might go one step on. But none of the linings had been touched and the rest of her clothes were clean.

It was predictable in its way. As Rosie Dunn was predictable. Textbook predictable. The last little thrill before she turned her attention elsewhere.

Sophie found her stomach swimming and she bent over the bowl and vomited.

She washed under a tap and felt better. She returned to the waiting room and waited.

She could guess what Elise Cadogan would do in New York. Or might do, in her penthouse. A front man for Rufus Stone. Impeccable as Elise Cadogan. Competent, cool. A good brain and mouth that would stay closed. She was white, Anglo-Saxon and Protestant.

As Elise Cadogan she would be beyond reproach in her

penthouse with her little boy, her beauty, her intelligence.

Sophie started to sniff. The change of climate, as Cliff predicted, was bringing on the cold she'd been fighting off. She gave in and sneezed and her nose began to run.

As she drifted off into a light sleep, she had a strange dream. It was of Rufus Stone and Rosie Dunn on top of a sandcastle they'd built. But the waves started to lap around the foundations and grew in force so that the foundations were eaten away. Rufus Stone and Rosie Dunn threw buckets of sand down from the top but nothing stopped the waves. Then Rosie Dunn started to scream and Rufus Stone smiled at her and took her hand. Then he vanished and Rosie Dunn was falling down down down, to a far away place.

Sophie woke up with a start, smoked a cigarette and waited for dawn.

At six the ground hostesses arrived.

At six thirty the small restaurant opened.

At seven the plane took off.

18

They sat, for a moment, in the airport carpark, Cliff's hands on the wheel, his fingers tapping out a noisy staccato.

'You saw her?' he finally asked.

Sophie nodded, hardly trusting herself to speak in case the tension gave way to tears. She turned away from Cliff's drawn face. He'd been through the hours too, counting each one off.

'So now it's all over?'

Had Sophie wanted to answer she couldn't have anyway. A jet taking off shook the air and Cliffie let out the clutch.

On the road through to the city he asked her again.

'Almost,' said Sophie.

'So it's home we go?'

Sophie shook her head. 'I want to make a call on someone down at Auburn.'

She put on her dark glasses. 'It's a question of conscience.'

'Who?'

'Just drive. Let me get myself together.'

'OK.' Cliff drove in silence. It was almost as difficult. 'How's Molly Meldrum?'

Cliff turned down towards Central Station and out to Parramatta. 'We slept together. Old Molly picked up things were bad. Slept down by my feet, under the blankets. Dunno how he managed it. I'd be asphixiated!'

'Your feet,' Sophie lit up a cigarette, 'not to mention other natural functions!'

The sun came out in a violent rush from behind the cumulus, red and swollen, hoping for a bit of aggro.

Cliff turned on to Parramatta Road and began the descent to the purgatorial regions of Sydney. House after brick house was followed by petrol station and Lebanese grocery shop, followed by acres of brick that might have been grocery shops or perhaps haberdashery shops. And pubs. Frequently pubs.

It all blurred the edges of Phuket and Rosie Dunn while Cliff drove faster to escape his origins, honking, braking, lane-changing.

'Dunno why they don't put an expressway through here. It's bloody dangerous for the pedestrians. Getting across the road, I mean. All those old Greek ladies need running shoes.'

'For Christ's sake Cliff, slow down. We've not got an appointment with God.'

'Thought it was. Thought it must be that old priest you trot down and visit once in a while.'

'It is.' Sophie leaned back and gave Cliff a bit of a grope. 'It is.'

'Miss me, eh?' Cliff looked pleased and slowed down, as they all did with more in the offing.

The glow lasted past more suburbs until, following Sophie's direction, Cliff turned left down a road and right over a railway bridge and past a convent, and left behind Parramatta Road with the towns astride it and gutted by its presence and the horizon, themselves only temporary clamps on an artery that must reach some heart far distant from them.

Ahead was the small wooden church with its belfry in brown, unpainted wood.

Cliff drew into the kerb. 'I'll go and find a cup of coffee.'
'Where?'

Cliff shrugged and stood on the accelerator.

Sophie watched while the blue Volkswagon disappeared around the corner, then wandered into the church.

Father Aquino was out of Calabria with a long line of undistinguished ancestors. He had weathered time and his

154

superiors and was gifted with the nearest thing to wisdom she knew.

Now and then a flash of its light came from the old bugger and hit you hard. He swore by garlic for the health and the presbytery usually bore witness to his faith. He was, by now, probably pickled for eternity in it.

That was another thing which had denied him promotion. That and his candour. Father Aquino was a child and like a child opened his mouth as he saw fit.

He had been Sophie's confessor, some lives ago, back in North Sydney and he had heard her first confession. She had begun with a few venial foibles then launched into the mortal efforts culled from a few books doing an illegal round at school – lecherous thoughts (mispronounced), not to mention concubinage, blasphemy and intoxication.

The pious litany had been interrupted, to Sophie's religious irritation, by a guffaw issuing from the confessional and Sophie had won a life-long admirer. It was a story the old man liked to repeat to her, mimicking the portentious saintly tones and high-flown fervour.

Sophie came back to herself, lit a candle, watched the flame flicker and stabilise. She didn't pray anything in particular but sniffed at the memory of incense, felt the presence of what once she would have called God but now knew to be her own interior stillness. It calmed other thoughts, as it always did, and only in this place.

The mirror of her judgement grew less cloudy. David was there at peace, in her. Rosie Dunn and Rufus Stone were there in their calm self love which dwelt in its own hell and felt no horror. Nothing. A gap in both. A missing neuron.

It was a pity indeed that Ruth Dunn's wish had not been mother to the act. Rosie Dunn would wait like a banked fire until the next time and the time after that. Nothing could be changed.

Every morn and every night some are born to sweet delight. Every night and every morn, some to wickedness are born. So had said Blake in words to that effect.

She crossed herself. The holy water stoop was almost dry but a few drops flicked on to her forehead.

The presbytery next door was approached by a small front garden where Father Aquino grew his herbs. The basil was now woody. Some aged tomato plants sheltered the thyme and sage while the rosemary flaunted itself over the rocks, cascading onto a polished brass front door. A few marigolds too, were still at it.

She lifted the polished knocker and let it fall.

The aged housekeeper, in respectable widow's black, opened the door. Her old black eyes stared out of a sallow skin and hadn't lost their bead.

Without a good-day she led the way along the linoleum-covered floor to the kitchen.

Father Aquino was sitting at the table, a book propped up against a loaf of bread. Probably one of those gnostic documents he specialised in.

'Sophie, cara mia.' He unbent himself, stood and delivered a smacking kiss on each cheek. 'A coffee?'

'A coffee, Signora. A coffee. Work woman, work!'

The signora moved slowly to the percolator, poured, added sugar without asking and rummaged for some biscuits in a painted jar.

Father Aquino closed the text with a wink. 'Almost as saucy as your first confession, my girl.'

They sat down, drank the coffee and exchanged pleasantries then Father Aquino checked the grounds in both their cups.

'In the village,' he checked again, 'there was a woman who divined from these. She was good on deaths and money. My mother swore by her.'

'Let's talk.'

Father Aquino recognised the tone of voice. 'We'll go to my study. If anyone calls, Mrs Mifsoud, I am not home. And, no listening at the door!'

Mrs Mifsoud stared at the well-polished coal stove.

'We like the food from it. Better flavour. We are an old-fashioned pair, aren't we Mrs Mifsoud?'

Mrs Mifsoud apparently didn't hear.

'Stubborn as a mule,' announced Father Aquino and led the way, leaving Mrs Mifsoud contemplating the now empty cups.

The study had two faded leather chairs, a desk with a Florentine leather top, a large bust of Thomas Aquinas and a new acquisition, a hand-carved Virgin eaten by termites. The faded rose gold and blue bespoke a culture that wasn't Ireland.

'It is from Gubbio, a present, a recent present. Late thirteenth century and smuggled in by a nun, termites and all,' announced Father Aquino, with obvious satisfaction at the good sister's anarchistic tendencies.

Sophie lit up a cigarette and the old man fumbled for his pipe and tobacco in his cassock pocket.

'It's a question of judgement, Father. A case I've been on. It's now more or less over. But there is a moral question. And you'll pick it up as I go along. Only one question of judgement that I can and must make, one way or the other.'

The old man puffed and sat back, pipe in hand, eyes looking somewhere beyond her at a point of eternity he was fast approaching.

'Go on, Sophie. Go on.'

Sophie began with the day of Rosie Dunn's inquest and that evening when Charlie Dunn, drunk and seeking revenge and truth, had accosted her on the *Queen Elizabeth*. The old man interrupted her to get details on Charlie Dunn and the food she'd eaten. The second to satisfy his own Italian curiosity.

The story wound on into dead ends and out again: Janet Craig, Ruth Dunn, Rosie. Then the unravelling and the truth of what had happened at the Gap. The drug world and what evidence she had. The execution of Jim Stokes. Sophia Mavrakis played with. Her own now admitted fear that indeed she herself would not survive. The horror of the face she had finally seen, up at the house above Kata Beach. The real story of Rosie Dunn and the real evil she had committed.

Sophie paused for breath. The old priest clicked his fingers then stood up, poured two glasses of wine donated by one of his Lebanese parishioners.

Sophie sipped and continued more calmly as she entered the old man's calm, where Janet Craig and Rosie Dunn in their embrace, Rosie Dunn and Rufus Stone in theirs, became abstract figures. Small, small, commonplaces under the eye of eternity.

'So,' said the old man, 'Rufus Stone runs, controls and bribes. He is a man who is an agent of evil. That is clear. As the girl is clear, although I have not met one like her.'

'She is also mother of her father's child. A fine son, Father Aquino.'

Father Aquino nodded.

'She is a woman that I can only imagine, even having met her. It's really only her acts that tell you. To look at her you would think a nice suburban Madonna was staring back at you. But, in fact, she's a de Sade woman. One of the women who run the castle in the *One Hundred and Twenty Days of Sodom*.'

'But she does not own death,' mentioned Father Aquino. 'Death owns death or perhaps God in some more ultimate sense.'

'Rufus Stone is an infant beside her potential – the emperor presiding over hell, selling off a generation for profit. They've always done that, though. There's nothing new in it, is there?'

'No, Sophie.'

'She is the stronger of the two. But he provides her with her field. And he will never in this society be caught. He will never ever face a judge.'

Father Aquino waited and then, in the silence, stood up, left the room and returned a moment later. He was carrying the morning paper. He unfolded it slowly, having the Italian sense of occasion.

'Read the front page, Sophie.'

Sophie felt herself going into a kind of shock. She stared at the headline and stared at the photo under it.

'Rufus Stone was called to account yesterday evening at around seven,' said Father Aquino, noting Sophie's eyes unmoving on the photograph. 'He is now accounting for every last sin, and the pain of every last person he has afflicted

158

for his rapacity to own this world. Now, Sophie, he owns
nothing. Only his soul. And on that, the Light of God is
now shining. It must be the most terrible of things for men
such as he. For them it is hell, Sophie.'

Sophie read slowly the two paragraphs with a promise of
an obituary on the middle page.

Rufus Stone had got up as normal and had been driven
over to Bondi Beach where despite the chill he had run and
then ridden the waves. He had returned home for breakfast
and had felt a little tired, according to his housekeeper. He
had put in a normal day's work and in the evening he had
gone to the local squash courts. Had played three games then,
while his partner was out getting a drink of water, had fallen
down.

He was dead on arrival at St Vincent's Hospital. A massive
coronary occlusion.

'And so,' said the old man, 'Miss Rosie Dunn is also dead.
You said that the trust in New York had not yet been set
up? That the apartment there was in Rufus Stone's name?
It has come, too, at a bad time for a woman bent on wickedness.
She is left without her field to play on, Sophie.

'She was, after all, only the concubine of an emperor.'

Sophie nodded.

'And too, Janet Craig is left to face herself. No one now
pays for her habit. No one calls her to come play on the
field of power. She, who was just a servant of this Rosie
Dunn, is also left. To face. Or, not to face.'

Sophie waited.

'And the only problem is now the sin of Charlie Dunn
and the knowledge of incest that his wife has. That is your
point of action Sophie, and that is why you've come to me.
For a little moral support, since you know what you must
do.'

Sophie nodded.

'There is only one way to deal with what Rosie Dunn
manipulated. There is always only one way to clean the wound
of the pus and dead flesh around it. To cauterise as surgeons
did even in my youth. Sometimes with a red-hot knife.

'Two souls, Charlie Dunn and Ruth Dunn must both face themselves and their daughter. One day, you see, she may wish to creep back. She would think of a story, Sophie. She would find a way back into her father's heart if not his bed. And he, the father, must face what he wished to happen, for Miss Rosie Dunn simply knew where the desire was, in him, in others, and fed that desire until from seed it came to flower.

'They must face themselves and their daughter. If they do not wish to, you at least have tried.'

Sophie stood up.

'And what will you do with the money Rufus Stone planted in your account, Sophie?'

Sophie smiled, for the first time in weeks, it felt. 'I know a small-time crim who isn't a crim. He has a gambling compulsion and he embezzled. After the trial I'll give him a cheque since they'll demand restitution. Just pray they don't gaol him, Father.'

'Good.' Father Aquino saw her out the front door, noted Cliff and waved. 'You never change, Sophie. Never in your heart. God will be pleased with you. Now, say a "Hail Mary" and say another when you drive to the Dunn house.'

Father Aquino opened the car door and Sophie got in. She squeezed the old man's hand then let go, since Cliff was in a hurry to hit Parramatta Road.

19

It was the morning of Jamey boy's trial.

Sophie was down at the Darlinghurst court-house standing under the intimidating neo-classical columns. Meant to express, Sophie supposed, the strength and durability of justice, they somehow looked like stodgy bourgeois legs carrying an ageing body. Besides, the roof under which she sheltered leaked like an old man's defective bladder. It more or less summed up the situation inside, too.

Sophie re-belted Cliff's flasher's mac and thought to move out and locate Jamey with the tribe of friends. Then she remembered Rufus Stone's funeral at ten that morning.

They had all been there: the judges, the editors, police chiefs and magistrates, industrialists and socialites, the Minister of Justice and the Federal Minister of Industry, a former wife in mourning with three former children. But not Rosie Dunn, stranded on a stationary ship up at Kata Beach, rocking to and fro with no current – yet.

Rufus Stone had been Church of England. At least, had been buried according to those rites, where God, as a superior upper-middle-class man, presided over another Eastern suburbs chap's sad demise. And St Andrew's Cathedral had mustered all the civil pomp that the Calvinists specialised in – a cathedral choir, a tame Bishop and a couple of lit candles.

The coffin had been closed, and tasteful red roses had lain

on the expensive wood. The sermon was masterly in its civic pomp and impregnable in its platitudes. Several people had yawned, including the former wife.

The coffin had come out to 'Thy Hand o God, has Guided, Thy Flock From Age to Age'. For a moment, Sophie thought she might get a fit of the giggles.

Then she saw Sean Long in a charcoal-grey suit, fixed him while her eye and forced him to look at her. And, outside among the milling guests, she'd got close.

'So it was a trade off. Rosie Dunn for Jim Stokes?'

Sean Long had nodded.

'You rotten shit,' she suggested quietly.

Sean Long shrugged and moved off away from the television cameras.

Sophie did the same, but for different reasons. She didn't want to speak to or acknowledge Charlie Dunn with wife Ruth mingling about; Charlie with his magnetic gaze fixed on the State Premier, no doubt an old buddy from Branston. Charlie seemed to be enjoying a joke of some kind, while Ruth smiled pleasantly to the wife and showed a good angle for the cameras should they move towards her.

Sophie came back to herself and actual life. She glanced at her watch. Jamey's trial was due to start in ten minutes. She made a dash for the entrance and wondered why the rain, which had held off for the Rufus Stone send-off, was pelting down now.

She found the old gang a moment later, milling about in a corridor that smelled of damp. Jamey boy was reserved in a dark suit and tie. Mary, his wife, in severe academic blouse and skirt. Lulu James, the novelist with the big boobs, sneezed and rustled about in her confessional dark crimson, hair neatly done back in a bun. It was a lifetime ago she'd dandled Jamey boy on her knees and breathed against that pretty white neck.

Lulu, so it seemed, had had a mass for Jamey's safety, but Lulu had been unable to catch Sophie, despite messages on the machine.

Sophie apologised as they walked into the court, rather

like a modern theatre, with the seats tiered so that the judge's chair and the tables for silks and solicitors under it were definitely on stage. Secondary to the theatre was the accused, now entering his box and giving his plea of Guilty.

Lulu shut up while the charges were being read. Forty thousand bucks could collect a long list of indictable offences.

'Are you being called?' Lulu asked Sophie.

'No. He pleaded guilty and the Silk didn't think a Private Dick was a relevant character witness for the accused.'

'Fascist pig,' muttered Lulu and got into the first decade of the Rosary.

It all went smoothly. Character witnesses, Gamblers Anonymous and a few others, but since lunchtime was drawing near, the Silk for Jamey boy wasn't going to delay matters.

The last was Mary, serene and articulate, and the Judge sat forward and listened intently to a young woman who talked in his language and explained the havoc of the compulsion on a marriage that had broken which both, now, were trying to heal. It was a masterly performance, and the Judge gently asked several questions and was satisfied by the replies.

Jamey boy in the meantime stared at the Judge. In fact, he hadn't taken his eyes off him. He was whiter around the gills than before, but his look was firm enough. Not that the Judge had looked at him. Not once. Sophie was unsure what to make of that sign and didn't have time to consider since Lulu had grabbed her hand. The Judge was sifting through his copious notes, underlining with his pen and finally looking up.

There was a moment's pause and the Judge looked at Jamey boy, considering him. Then he made his statement.

'You are a good man,' he said. 'You are not a criminal and not a wicked man.'

Lulu released Sophie's hand, found a white lace handkerchief that had seen better days and began to blubber.

'Three years' suspended sentence,' concluded the Judge, 'and a weekly restitution of one hundred dollars. For the following three years you will do weekend community work, which I am sure will please you as a means of showing your new sincerity of heart.'

'Jesus and Mary,' muttered Lulu. 'Where does that old prick come from?'

They trooped out – Daph Cowlie of the balloon body and skinny legs, Jim and Bert and Dave and Sonia and Angela and the rest.

'Let's go to the pub and celebrate,' suggested Daph, and Jamey boy, floating nowhere in particular, was sucked into the situation and disgorged with them down the road, where the Mental Bondage clerks drank up large.

Jamey boy sat while the drinks were brought over, and the Silk, in a hurry for lunch, played nicely with the compliments.

Mary ordered a dry sherry.

Still in role, thought Sophie. A brilliant performance.

'So, you're getting back together?' Sophie drank deep on her pint of bitter.

'Not bloody likely,' Mary swigged down her sherry. 'I've found a beaut new man. A lecturer in anthropology.'

Jamey boy heard the remark and looked sombre. The moment, decided Sophie, had obviously arrived.

'Well Jamey,' said Sophie in a loud voice, loving every minute of Fairy Godmother and Lady Bountiful, 'to start off the benefit, I've got some good news for you.' She handed over the envelope.

Jamey boy opened it. Stared at the cheque.

'Jesus, Soph – thirty thousand dollars!'

'And the rest you'll find yourself. But you'll be well forward with repayments. Quite enough to go back to university.'

Jamey boy broke down and started to bubble. Lulu took his hand and bubbled too.

The others cheered and drank up.

'You really trust me!' Jamey boy managed to get out.

'And who, Jamey boy, is the cheque made out to?'

Jamey looked harder and grinned. 'Rental Bond Board.'

'With a covering letter.' Sophie stood up and the Silk used her move to make his own escape. Sophie also left. She had one last job to do.

She arrived at her car, got in, and drove. Then she remembered Father Aquino's advice.

She began the angelic salutation in Latin, which was how she had learned it as a child.

20

It was Charlie Dunn who opened the front door, an early sherry in his hand.

'Finally seen the papers, have you?' asked Charlie. 'Rufus Stone is dead.' Charlie smiled. 'The mills of God grind slow.'

He stood aside and let Sophie in.

'Ruth's outside, in the garden. She's had the eucalypt taken down and is planting a giant magnolia. It'll make a good display in summer, so old Ruth reckons.'

It made it harder, Charlie Dunn's cocky jocularity.

Sophie avoided the picture windows that framed Ruth Dunn in old slacks and a windbreaker supervising some men as they cut up the gumtree and another dug a hole for a large magnolia awaiting transplant.

Charlie raised his glass, and Sophie found the ice dissolving and a slow hot anger circulating where it had been.

'It's not an occasion for celebration, Charlie.'

'Oh yes, it is.' Charlie poured her a sherry. 'That bastard's hit the dust. No need now to think of a contract. It's been taken out and the work done, so to speak.'

'I want to see Rosie Dunn's room.' Sophie walked towards the stairs. Charlie followed her.

'We brought back everything from her flat at the Cross. So those bloody burglars got nothing. Safe would have been empty, anyway.

'Here it is,' Charlie quietened down. 'This is Rosie's room.'

They stood in the doorway.

It was calm, still, in there, facing on to the garden. The noise of the chainsaw from some other world. For this, Sophie recognised from her Catholic soul, was a shrine.

'Who looks after the room, Charlie?' asked Sophie at her gentlest.

Charlie swilled around his sherry. 'I do. Ruth says we should throw away all the stuff. Clothes, books, the lot, have the room painted. But I won't have that and I clean it. Ruth doesn't believe in keeping memory green.'

Sophie walked into the room on Charlie Dunn's quiet intensity. There was a large three-quarter bed where Rosie Dunn had led her drunken rugby prop father who'd never much grown beyond that game, and there she'd taken off her clothes and pulled him to her.

Sophie sat down on it and touched the supersize teddy bear.

'I'd prefer you sat on the easy chair, Sophie.'

There was no need for any confirmation, but it was given anyway, in that voice.

Sophie lit up a cigarette, the first act of profanation of the shrine.

Charlie was staring at the bookcase. Sophie stared at the form photos, the prefect's photo, the pictures of the beach house up the coast with Rosie and Charlie together.

'I'd like her thesis back, soon, Sophie.' Charlie sat instead on the chair. 'I want to re-read it.'

Sophie nodded.

'Why have you come today?' Charlie leaned forward.

'You asked me to find out whatever happened to Rosie Dunn. The report is complete. The case is over, Charlie. If you want, after I finish telling you, I'll type it out for you.'

Charlie stared at the photos, and because of the tears in his eyes it was made, somehow, easier.

Sophie gently and carefully led Charlie Dunn through the case. Point by point she outlined what she knew and what had happened.

She waited for the shock, and it came and the disbelief. She produced the photos. She talked again of Rufus Stone.

She came to the final chapter up at Kata Beach, with Rosie Dunn and her son, and Charlie's son.

She hit harder then, and again harder for Charlie Dunn needed now, while white hot with this knowledge, to be stamped with what Rosie Dunn was.

She finished. She did not look at him.

'Now, Charlie, I'll go downstairs. All that I've told you Ruth will be forced to confirm. You see, I have tapes of her conversations, Janet Craig's conversations, other people's conversations.'

She left the room, went down the stairs and out to the garden. Ruth saw her coming and perhaps from the way Sophie walked or the look on her face, she knew before Sophie opened her mouth.

'Where is he?' she asked.

'Inside, Ruth. He knows everything. Everything, Ruth. That was my brief. The brief is now fulfilled.'

Sophie sat in a garden chair and waited. Half an hour passed and Charlie Dunn came down the stairs with his wife and went with her to the sofa.

Sophie waited again.

Dusk was falling before Ruth stood at the French windows. Sophie got up and walked into the room.

Then Ruth made a mistake. She handed Sophie a cheque. Sophie looked at it. It was for the other twenty thousand.

Sophie studied Charlie Dunn's firm signature. Then she ripped the cheque in two and handed it back.

Ruth Dunn looked at the pieces of the cheque then went and threw them on the fire.

'I'll ring the Smith Family tomorrow,' Ruth said to Charlie. 'They can come for Rosie's clothes and, and, the bed and clothing. Her books need not go to charity. I'm sure the school library will find a use for them.'

Sophie allowed herself to look at Charlie Dunn, white of face but rallying.

'Well,' went on Ruth, 'now we know how she died. Up in Thailand. What was the name of the beach?'

Sophie told her again.

'Kata Beach,' said Ruth Dunn. 'I don't suppose any of us will be taking holidays up there.'

Sophie lit a Gauloise from an old packet to get the taste out of her mouth. 'I think I'd better go now.'

Charlie Dunn stayed where he was, pinned to the sofa and Ruth Dunn.

'I was very sorry about your brother, David. I did try to tell you, that day up at the bookshop. I wonder what will happen to her?'

'I expect her business associates will give her a widow's pension.'

Ruth essayed a small wintery smile at the notion. And opened the front door. 'I will tell the other two, about Rosie, their sister. It's the only real protection for us, isn't it? Truth!'

'All?' asked Sophie.

Ruth had already locked Charlie and Rosie away in a cupboard and for a moment had to consider what Sophie meant. Then her lips thinned.

'No, none of that. The rest will be sufficient for the children. And should she try and contact them and make claim to her relationship with Charlie, they will simply disbelieve. They will see it as part of her malicious destructive nature. Just a part of Rosie Dunn's illness. Of her madness and wickedness. She is a very wicked girl, you know.'

'Yes,' said Sophie. 'She is.'

Sophie walked out to the street gate and behind her Ruth Dunn didn't wait to see her off the premises before shutting the house door.

Cliff, faithful Cliff, was snoozing in the Volkswagon and woke up as she got in.

'OK Soph?'

'OK.' Sophie leaned back. 'Home Cliff. A hot bath and then sleep and more sleep.'

'OK Soph.' Cliff turned on the ignition.

Sophie closed her eyes and Cliff drove with one hand, the other holding her against him.

Jamie +
8 Harry Bowers.

   Edison Charlie Dunn
17 Everything goes back to Rufus Stone (first real
                                        introduction)
19 The killing of her brother David.
22 Janet Craig.
25 Rosie Dunn & Rufus Stone / Ruth
27 Marjorie, "Charlie's former sister-in-law".
* 28 Marjorie "Family don't bother telling you who they
      are. They're really just part of the jigsaw
      pattern. It's only when they're gone you look at
      the empty space and wonder."
   32 Janet Craig / shooting up.